"DON'T BE RIDICULOUS. WOMEN SHOULDN'T RACE."

"Anyone who rides a horse well and enjoys the sport should race," Margaret countered. "And while I dislike bragging, I have to admit I ride quite well. You've just finished telling me how well you ride. The path lies open. Let's race."

Thomas could feel the desire building inside him to do just that. He forced himself to frown. "Miss Munroe, if you have no care for your own safety, I must. I cannot race with you."

"If I were a man you'd race with me," she accused.

"If you were a man," Thomas snapped, "I wouldn't be out riding with you at this ungodly hour!"

She glared at him. "So sorry to have inconvenienced you, my lord. I assure you it won't happen again. Pray do not let us detain you." She tightened her grip on the reins and pressed her heels into the flanks of the black. Aeolus flattened his ears and broke into a gallop onto The Row.

Thomas gritted his teeth. He scolded himself for his lack of will power. He pressed the Arabian into a gallop and tore off after her.

Other Books by Regina Scott

THE UNFLAPPABLE MISS FAIRCHILD

THE TWELVE DAYS OF CHRISTMAS

"SWEETER THAN CANDY" in
A MATCH FOR MOTHER

THE BLUESTOCKING ON HIS KNEE

"A PLACE BY THE FIRE" in
MISTLETOE KITTENS

CATCH OF THE SEASON

A DANGEROUS DALLIANCE

Published by Zebra Books

THE MARQUIS' KISS

Regina Scott

ZEBRA BOOKS
Kensington Publishing Corp.
http://www.zebrabooks.com

ZEBRA BOOKS are published by

Kensington Publishing Corp.
850 Third Avenue
New York, NY 10022

First Printing: October, 2000
10 9 8 7 6 5 4 3 2 1

Printed in the United States of America

To Meryl, a heroine for this and any other century

One

Thomas, Marquis DeGuis, stood before his host's well-stocked liquor cabinet and, for the first time in his life, considered getting roaring drunk. As he never did anything in excess, he wasn't entirely sure how much he would need to consume to render himself unconscious. Nor was he certain how long it might take. There lay the rub. The only reason to get drunk was to obliterate the last few minutes, and the sooner, the better.

Unfortunately, the firelight reflecting in the depths of the fine liquors only made him remember the fire of contempt in Lady Janice Willstencraft's green eyes when she had refused him.

"A sorry performance, my lord," she had sneered. "Do you truly think I would agree to marry anything less than a real man?"

He shut his eyes against the memory. He would be very tempted to put the whole horrid scene down to a case of pre-wedding jitters on his part. Only this was the second time it had happened.

The faintest of noises caused him to snap his eyes open and glare about the study. The darkly paneled room, so far down the corridor from the ballroom, had seemed an excellent escape from the crowds attending the Baminger's ball. He detested gossip, and returning to the room without the lady on his arm would cause just that. He would have to make his farewells of his host eventually, but for the moment a quiet place to think had been more welcome. Now the gold velvet drapes, closed over the twin windows, looked like a perfect hiding place for some trysting couple, or a gossip-hungry guest.

"Is anyone there?" Thomas demanded.

There was a decided snort from the vicinity of the nearby sofa. Thomas watched as a head bobbed into view over the back. Two startled blue eyes blinked at him under a thatch of straw-colored hair. Blinked, and then widened fatuously.

Thomas smothered a groan and strode for the door, clipping out his regrets with equal haste. "Sorry to have disturbed you, Pinstin. My mistake. Another time."

He wasn't fast enough. Reginald Pinstin, related to half the best families of England and avoided by most of them, leapt off the sofa and scurried to intercept him. "My lord, my Lord DeGuis," he implored in his reedy voice, neatly blocking the way to freedom. "No harm done! Please, join me for a chat. It has been an age."

Thomas kept a polite smile in place while he sorted through options to rid himself of the fellow. Pinstin had a legendary way of turning rejection into gossip. The normal expressions of regret would never work.

"Yes, it has been a while," Thomas allowed. "But I was just about to leave."

Pinstin cocked his impish face, giving his linen cravat another wrinkling after the sofa. "But my lord," he protested, smiling coyly, "are not congratulations in order? I understood you were to offer for the fair lady tonight."

As usual, Pinstin's sources were infallible. Thomas

kept his face composed. There was no mistaking the patent desire in Pinstin's pale blue eyes. The fellow could hardly breathe he was so anxious to be the first to hear the news, and the first to spread it. His gloved hands clasped and unclasped before his brown velvet coat and breeches.

"Come now," Pinstin urged as Thomas hesitated. "Don't keep the tidings to yourself. Is Lady Janice off somewhere showing the DeGuis diamond to a few choice friends?"

Thomas had to answer the question, yet he could not bring himself to lie, even to a gossip like Pinstin. Nor could he admit the truth. The man's familiarity was cloying; his pity would be unthinkable.

"Perhaps you should ask the lady," he suggested, attempting to pass the fellow. Pinstin, shorter and thinner, was also surprisingly quick on his feet, easily dancing to block his way. For an instant Thomas wondered whether he had it in himself to strike the fellow, his fists curling at the idea. His conscience was appalled by the thought, even more appalled than it had been over his desire to drink himself into a stupor. A DeGuis did not display his emotions in public. He clearly needed to take himself in hand.

Pinstin must have sensed the struggle, for his eyes lightened. "Is there something you want to say, my lord?" he asked with an encouraging smile. "Shall we drink a toast to your happiness?"

At the moment, Thomas' only chance at happiness lay beyond the yawning door. As if in answer to his unspoken prayer, his friend, Courtney Dellington, Viscount Darton, strode past.

"Lord Darton," he called, annoyed that his voice had the hint of desperation. "In here. A moment of your time."

Pinstin spun, and Thomas could feel his eagerness

increase again as the viscount filled the doorway. Court's welcoming smile froze on his face at the sight of the gossip, but he recovered nicely. As Thomas had hoped, he recognized the situation immediately.

"There you are, DeGuis," he said with just the right amount of pique in his controlled voice. "Your sister has been looking for you for an age. I'm sure you'll excuse us, Pinstin. Wouldn't want to keep the lady waiting."

"No indeed, no indeed," Pinstin warbled. "A lovely woman, Lady Catherine. So modest, so self-effacing. I shall soon be wishing you happy as well, eh, Lord Darton?"

Court raised a quizzing glass from his evening black and eyed Reggie as if he'd developed spots. As few boasted the iron-brown eyes of the viscount, few could use the move to such advantage. It also did not hurt that the viscount was an Englishman's Englishman—tall, blond, clean-jawed, and strong-limbed. He had so impressed Thomas, in fact, that he had arranged for the fellow to marry his younger sister Catherine, although he had not yet broached the subject with his sister. Even with Pinstin's noted abilities to ferret out the truth, he was more than a little surprised that the little tattle-monger had guessed about the arrangement. Time for him and Court to beat a retreat while they still shared a few secrets.

"Excuse us," Thomas said pointedly, managing to out-maneuver the fellow at last. Pinstin, shaking off the effects of the viscount's glare, scurried to the liquor cabinet.

"A toast," he proclaimed, fumbling with the crystal goblets and a decanter of brandy. "To Lady Catherine DeGuis."

Court froze, and Thomas was forced to halt.

"He has us there," the viscount murmured for him

alone. "Can you hear the ton when he tells everyone we refused to honor your sister?"

"There's a reason he's dreaded," Thomas growled back. "Let's get this over with."

As one, they strode back to the cabinet to accept the goblets Pinstin poured for them with hands that visibly shook in his eagerness. Thomas took the barest of sips. Court threw back a mouthful. Pinstin guzzled his and reached hastily for the decanter.

"And to Lady Janice Willstencraft," he said, refilling his glass and topping off Court's. "Soon to be Lady DeGuis."

The two drank again, but Thomas set his goblet quietly down on the cabinet. "And now we must leave," he said firmly.

Pinstin frowned. "But my lord," he all but whined, "you did not drink to your lovely bride."

Curse the fellow for his sharp eyes and curse his own inability to lie. Even Court was looking at him with the slightest of frowns. He would have loved to fob them off with generalities, but he could not dance around the truth forever. Better to get it over with. "She turned me down."

Court had the good manners merely to blink. Pinstin went so far as to gasp.

"That's impossible," he declared. "All the wagers have been placed. She's been seen riding with you twice in one week. She allowed you to escort her to any number of balls. She can't have turned you down. My God, Lord DeGuis, you're the catch of the Season!"

"Apparently not everyone agrees," Thomas replied. The man's disbelief was almost as disgusting as the expected pity. Apparently this evening was a trial he was meant to endure. Funny—he had always considered he had developed enough character.

The trial was not nearly over. Like some newly shin-
gled attorney, Pinstin dragged out all the facts why
Lady Janice could not possibly have refused him.

"Your family name is as old as the Norman Con-
quest," he chided. "It's well-known your estate is
worth thirty thousand pounds per annum, enough
to purchase a small country and more than enough
to satisfy the most spendthrift of wives. You're intelligent, well spoken, and a staunch Tory. At thirty-and-
two, you're not even ancient!"

"Certainly not," the twenty-eight-year-old Court
seemed to feel compelled to remark.

"Your health may be questionable given the
DeGuis tendency toward heart trouble," Pinstin continued. "But as you have not had an attack, I do not
see how anyone would not agree that you are a perfect specimen."

Thomas exchanged glances with Court, thankful
that for once Pinstin did not know everything. Apparently last December's attack remained a secret.

"Women," Court said with an exaggerated sigh,
obviously trying to put the fellow off the scent. Pinstin eagerly refilled the viscount's glass and his own.
"I daresay they can be far more demanding than the
most temperamental of horses. Of course, I do not
include Lady Catherine DeGuis in that assessment,"
he hurriedly added as Pinstin leaned forward, nose
twitching as if he caught the hint of scandal.

"And again to Lady Catherine!" Pinstin declared,
rising his glass yet again. "That paragon who is never
effusive, never emotional. What a shame the other
women of the ton are not more like her."

"Here, here," Court agreed with more enthusiasm
than Thomas had seen in him. He was forced to re-
trieve the glass and take another sip, when in fact he
actually found his sister a little too quiet. He could

seldom fathom how she felt on a particular subject
and had given up trying years ago. The only strong
attachment he had seen was her devotion to their
elderly aunt Lady Agnes DeGuis. The only fair-haired
DeGuis in several generations, Catherine appeared
almost colorless at times. As he loved her dearly, her
reticence and reserve was a matter that concerned
and perplexed him. Still, he was pleased the young
viscount liked her as he had hoped. Now if only he
could put his own life in order.

"And to gentle ladies everywhere," Pinstin continued magnanimously, sloshing drink on the inlaid
wood of the cabinet as he refilled his glass. "May
Lord DeGuis soon find one to his liking. I ask you,"
he waved at the gilt-framed mirror over the fireplace,
"what woman in her right mind would refuse that?"

Thomas spared a brief glance in the mirror. He
supposed that in his own way, he cut as good a figure
as Court did. He was taller than most of the men of
his circle and well-muscled. His short-cut hair was a
shiny black. His piercing blue eyes and chiseled features had served him well when putting his oppo-
nents in place during Parliamentary debates.
Catherine had said he had a noble chin, whatever
that meant. He could see nothing to make Lady
Janice suddenly take him in such disdain. But then,
it wasn't how he looked but how he performed certain functions that seemed to be his undoing. He
schooled his face to impassivity to hide the frustration
the thought caused him. Perhaps if he remained his
usual composed self for the few minutes it would take
to make his excuses to his host, he might survive this
ball with his dignity intact.

"It simply isn't fair," Pinstin protested, and
Thomas noticed with a frown that the goblet had
been emptied and filled yet again. "You're the para-

gon of paragons, and you get refused." He swallowed the brandy in one gulp and slammed the glass onto the top of the polished maple cabinet. "Well, we'll have no more of that! We'll beat this, even as Wellington beat Napoleon on the Peninsula."

Pinstin seized his arm. Thomas' frown deepened at the overly familiar gesture, but that didn't stop Pinstin from attempting to tow him to the study door. As it got him closer to freedom, he decided not to protest. Court set his glass down and strolled after him. The half smile on his face indicated he had imbibed just enough to find Thomas' predicament amusing.

"Take heart, man!" Pinstin was urging. "If Lady Janice won't have you, it is her loss. There is an entire ballroom of women just like her waiting for your attentions."

As if to belie his words, from down the corridor came the sound of someone laughing. The laugh was deep-throated and hiccoughing, as if the person was absolutely overcome with mirth. Court frowned but Thomas found it impossible not to smile. Someone at least was enjoying themselves tonight. He wished them well.

Pinstin had paled and frozen at the sound. Thomas removed his arm from the fellow's suddenly slack grip. "Thank you for your concern, Pinstin, but I think I'd rather not try my luck again so soon. I'll have my carriage brought around. Lord Darton, I trust you can see Lady Catherine home?"

Court nodded, moving around them for the door. Thomas realized belatedly that he had given the viscount an opportunity for escape, an opportunity his friend lost no time in taking. He didn't even look guilty about leaving Thomas standing next to a still-frowning Pinstin. The look in those cool brown eyes could only have been called relieved. Thomas executed a bow that managed to take him a little farther from Pinstin and turned to go.

"Wait," Pinstin hissed. The urgency in his voice pulled Thomas up short, but just for a moment. It could only be another trick. He took another two steps and found Pinstin at his elbow.

"Wait, my lord, please," Pinstin whined, scurrying to keep up as Thomas lengthened his strides. "I think I have the answer to your problems."

"Somehow, I doubt that," Thomas replied, refusing to halt. He could see the ballroom coming up on his left and ahead of it, the grand entryway.

"No, truly," Pinstin protested, shameless in his pursuit. "Perhaps you've chosen the wrong kind of women. After all, this is the second one to refuse you in the last eight months."

Any thought of charity for the fellow vanished. Thomas stopped and affixed him with a glare to equal Court's. "I certainly hope," he said in his most chilling tones, "that my other acquaintances are more forgetful or more tactful, sirrah."

"They won't be," Pinstin replied, obviously too foxed to see the danger signs. "Allison Munroe was nearly the belle of the season last year. No one could ever believe she preferred that country bumpkin she wed to you. Now, with Lady Janice turning you down as well, people are bound to talk."

"They may talk all they like," Thomas replied, resuming his pace. "But I am finished with discussing this topic this evening. Good night, Mr. Pinstin."

Pinstin started to protest, but Thomas refused to let the fellow stop him a second time. A man could only take so much abuse, and he had had more than his share this night. All he wanted was to leave. Before he could reach the entryway, the laugh came again from the ballroom, but this time it grated on his nerves, as if all one hundred of the Baminger's exalted guests had joined together to mock him. Despite himself, he drew up short. "Who the devil is that?"

His pause allowed Pinstin to catch up with him. "That's my cousin, Miss Margaret Munroe. You've met her. She's related to your past fiancée, Miss Allison Munroe. Now there's a woman who wouldn't turn you down. She's an Original, a kind use of the term, I assure you, but eminently suited to your needs."

Thomas had no interest in hearing about Pinstin's cousin, related to his past love or not. "I told you, Mr. Pinstin, I am no longer in the petticoat line. If you persist in this conversation, I shall be forced to plant you a facer."

Pinstin blinked, then his eagerness heightened. "You would strike me, my lord? You, who are so noted for his composure? This is unseemly. Lady Janice must have been vicious. You should try my cousin. She is a bruising rider, not unlike yourself. She dances divinely. She has an intriguing sense of humor."

He had no idea why, but Thomas found himself hesitating. Another time, he was sure Pinstin would have been delighted in the way his news had snared Thomas at last. Now the fellow was positively sweating to introduce him to his cousin.

"All right, Pinstin," he allowed. "You have been sufficiently interesting that you have my attention. If your cousin is such a paragon, why is she unwed?"

Pinstin appeared to be struggling with himself. His mouth opened and closed soundlessly, like an ornamental fish in a bowl, and he tightened his cravat until Thomas thought the fold would surely strangle him. "I, I really cannot say, my lord," he managed at last, although the sweat on his narrow brow attested to the fact that he wanted to say something very much. "She might be considered a bit odd by some, I suppose. She is nothing like the society belles you've chosen to pursue. You might say my cousin is the farthest thing from a belle while still remaining in polite society. But that should not be seen as a detriment. She is from the poorer side of the Munroe family, in wealth, beauty, and number of beaus. Anyone with such deficits would surely welcome the attentions of so presentable a suitor as yourself."

The fellow could not even refrain from gossiping about his own cousin, even when trying to arrange an introduction. Thomas shook his head in disgust. He didn't much like the way the fellow was maligning Miss Munroe. He also didn't like being told that a woman with severe social deficits was all he could get as a bride. As if he needed to find some ape leader, some maladroit, lackluster, impoverished spinster to fawn over him. The very idea made his bile rise. Surely there existed some intelligent, talented, beautiful woman of breeding who would be as pleased to marry him as he would be to ask her. Why should he settle for less?

Pinstin obviously took his brooding silence for agreement, for he seized Thomas' arm again. "She's perfect, I tell you, a complete contrast to Lady Janice. I'll introduce you, and you can see for yourself."

Horrified, Thomas attempted to remove himself from the fellow's clutches even as Pinstin drew him inexorably toward the nearby ballroom door. He had no interest in starting another courtship after the dismal endings of his last two. He certainly had no interest in meeting the Original Miss Munroe. And he had absolutely no interest in appearing in public on the arm of a mad man. But it was too late. Just as he managed to disengage his arm, Pinstin stumbled against him, forcing him through the open door and straight into the arms of Margaret Munroe.

Two

Margaret Munroe had not been having a particularly enjoyable evening. At her stepmother's insistence, she had agreed to allow the woman's nephew Reginald Pinstin to escort her to the Baminger ball. Margaret adored dancing; it was one of the three greatest loves of her life. Unfortunately, she had little use for Reggie. Narrow of face, mind, and character, the gangly fellow could not be counted on to comport himself in any manner resembling usefulness. His family, her family, had forced him into escorting her, but they could not make him dance with her. As it was, the makebait had circulated through the ballroom in search of gossip, claiming a sore foot and a weak back and any other ailment to prevent him from having to take the floor. As soon as she had gone to fetch herself some refreshment, he had disappeared. If she intended to dance that night, she would have to hunt for better game.

She had spotted several of her companions in the press of the entryway earlier and now gladly left the ballroom to find them. While she could not state that she currently had a single suitor, she did have a solid set of gentlemen who admired her. She scouted out Robbie Whattling, who was always willing to make a cake of himself. Dark haired and dark eyed, he had the same double-edged personality as Byron—joyous one moment, dejected the next. She was usually able to bring him out of the darkness. Tonight, however, he was already deep into a card game with the odious George Safton and unwilling to be disturbed even to dance with her. Safton cast her one of his venom-tipped glances that had earned him the appellation of The Snake, but she ignored him. She had already warned Robbie twice that the man was no good. She did not intend to waste her breath a third time.

She ran down Chas Prestwick, with whom her step-mother generally refused to let her dance, for all that he was heavenly on his feet. True to the reputation her stepmother feared, he was attempting a tryst with their host's oldest daughter Belinda. Of course, Mar-garet hadn't realized it until she had cornered Chas in the fire-lit sitting room next door to the study. She hadn't even glanced at the nearby sofa to notice Be-linda reclining there expectantly. She had been half-way through her explanation to Chas when the silly chit had sat up and glared at her. Chas had burst out laughing at Margaret's maladroit attempts to extri-cate herself from the situation. Margaret had laughed with him. Belinda Baminger had leaped to her feet and stalked off in a huff, threatening like an irra-tional child to tell her father, who would only have had to call Chas out. Poor Chas had had to decamp before Margaret had gotten so much as a country dance. Still, his parting wink in the ballroom door had made her laugh again.

She wandered back inside, hoping she might see someone else she recognized. It wasn't a large room, and half the guests were safely ensconced in the card room next door. Of the fifty or so people left, a few lounged on the sofas lining the narrow, satin-draped walls and most were on the parquet dance floor. Couples were moving through the steps of a country dance, silks and jewels glinting in the lights of the dual chandeliers overhead. Their movements were so slow and wooden that she wanted to scream in vexation. Was there no one in all this house who knew how to enjoy life?

She stalked around the edge of the floor, feeling like a hungry lioness forced to watch a herd of fat gazelle. Reggie was nowhere to be seen. He had either exhausted his limited appeal and was curled up on another sofa somewhere asleep or had found some pompous personage to flatter and cajole into revealing a tantalizing secret, as was his specialty. That was one thing she could say about her cousin— he was a marvelous little gossip. She didn't much admire the trait in general, but she appreciated anyone who used their gifts to advantage, especially gifts she did not possess.

And she made a hideous toady. For one thing, she lacked the tact necessary to excel at flattering her betters. For another, she had to contend with an honest streak and an appreciation of absurdity. Of course, right at the moment, she found it hard to appreciate her situation. Her stepmother had insisted that she wear an awful pink satin gown that washed out her dark coloring even as the puffy flounces along the neckline and hem made her look as if she were about to take flight. It was the outfit of a simpering girl fresh from the schoolroom, and not a mature young lady who was almost done weathering four full Seasons. Dressed so hideously, pressed into her cousin's company, forced to watch while others danced, was there anything that could go well about this night?

She completed her circle of the dance floor and approached a group of older people watching the dancers as she was. One of the gentlemen, a staunch military fellow, the Earl of Rillson, stiffened as she approached. Refusing to meet her eye, he excused himself from the group and scurried away, face going nearly as pale as his white mustache. She vaguely remembered recently telling him he looked very well for a man of his age and habits. Was she to blame that he had liver spots and gout? Her stepmother had had apoplexy.

"Honestly, Margaret," she had chastised as soon as the embarrassed man was out of earshot, "can you never think before you speak? How am I to find you a husband if you cannot behave in a civilized fashion?"

That was the problem, of course. The second Mrs. Munroe was determined that Margaret not waste her fourth Season. Having married Margaret's widowed father when Margaret was seventeen, the second Mrs. Munroe had immediately set about to prove she was the perfect society matron and just as good at arranging parties as the renowned Mrs. Ermintrude Munroe, Margaret's aunt. Aunt Ermintrude was a legend for her good taste and impeccable breeding. Her one area of failure was that her daughters had not married well. Therefore, it was imperative that Mrs. Helen Munroe do better by Margaret. The quest had cost Helen over five years so far. With her reputation at stake, she was getting desperate. Margaret must find a husband, before the end of the Season, which was only six weeks away.

To do her stepmother justice, Margaret tried to remember that the relentless prodding toward finding a mate came from a firm belief that the only way to happiness was marriage. All women married; that was how one lived. No Munroe had ever remained a spinster; it was unthinkable. Helen could not be so ignoble as to fail in this sacred duty.

Unfortunately for her stepmother, Margaret was equally certain that marriage would doom her to misery. She was smart enough to recognize that she had little in common with most young ladies her age. They minced through dances as if afraid to wrinkle their gowns; she gave herself over to the joy of the music. They perched on horseback and trotted along flower-bordered paths. She donned breeches in the country and slung herself across saddles built for men to pound across open fields. Only in London did she succumb to her stepmother's pleas to wear a riding habit and ride side saddle. While the other London ladies paid house calls on each other and congratulated themselves on their proper breeding, she spent her days looking for the most despised of citizens and helping them return to useful roles in society. Her stepmother despaired of her. Even her father prophesied that only a husband would curb her strange tendencies. Yet, if her father and stepmother could not appreciate her many eccentricities, how could she expect a husband to understand her?

Not that she abhorred the male sex in any way. That was one thing she shared with the other young ladies here for the Season—a healthy fascination with the male. She certainly couldn't dance without one, and it was much more fun to race when she was racing against one. True, some of the more stuffy gentlemen seemed appalled by her antics. Viscount Darton, whom she had beaten soundly in a private race last year, was a good example of that breed. He preferred his young ladies docile and colorless. A woman who could best him in anything clearly confused and frightened him. She'd never forget how stunned he'd looked at the end of the race when she'd peeled off the coachman's cape to reveal herself. It still smarted that her father had made her return the mare she had fairly won.

"We can't have people talking," he had scolded her. "You're a fine girl, Margaret, but some fellows can't abide a girl who shows them up. I know the Bible talks about not hiding our lights under a basket, but sometimes it's perfectly all right to tone down the brightness."

She, of course, did not agree, but she loved her father too much to argue about something so trivial. She had a wonderful thoroughbred gelding named Aeolus, far better than the three-year-old mare. The horse had gone home.

Much as she disliked the self-important types like Viscount Darton, however, there were any number of gentlemen she had met last year and this who were intelligent and had some appreciation for the activities she found interesting. Lord Leslie Petersborough was nearly as good a rider as she was, even if he couldn't win a carriage race over Chas Prestwick. Chas Prestwick was always up for an adventure, although she had to be careful not to let their adventures become known. The curricle race to Lincoln's Inn Fields last month had nearly cost her a week of dancing before she was able to convince her father that no one else would have recognized the groom at the back of the curricle as her.

Then there were the Whattlings. She had only managed to wind Robbie in a dance once and he had been foxed at the time. He was in such good shape from boxing, she knew. Of course, she also couldn't admit to have seen several of his bouts. Ladies did not watch boxing matches. His older brother Kevin, on the other hand, would never have danced with her, but was always willing to help fund her charities. He was especially kind to the abandoned ladies at

Comfort House, her latest pet project. If only he had been nobly born, then he might have been able to fight the bill Leslie had told her was brewing in the House of Lords to amend the Poor Laws. The wording of the bill might spell doom for her charitable efforts. But Leslie had yet to ascend to his title, and none of her other gentlemen friends were likely to hold seats on Parliament. Still, they were fine fellows and seemed to enjoy her company as much as she enjoyed theirs. Yet none of them would have considered courting her, much less marrying her.

Nor would she have considered marrying them. They clearly had other ideas about what a woman should be than what she was. Sometimes she thought they saw her as a younger sister; other times she wasn't sure they saw her as female at all. The fact did not trouble her. She had had enough fellows ogle her figure to know she had some attraction. She was just as glad she did not have to worry about breaking any of her comrades' hearts. It made enjoying their company so much easier.

Besides, she could hardly marry them when she was in love with someone else. None of them knew that; she had never even told her father or stepmother. It had happened suddenly, at the very beginning of the Season last year. She had always read of love at first sight, but she had never credited it would happen to her. Yet she had gone to the ball, looked across the ballroom, and known that the only man she would ever love was standing there.

He was perfect. That both excited and depressed her. What must it be like to be loved by the most intelligent, handsome man in London? And why would such a paragon ever notice the unconventional Miss Margaret Munroe? True, he raced. She had watched any number of his races since then,

cheering for him. He had not noticed. He also
danced, yet he had never asked her to dance. She
had been in his company any number of times, in
fact, and he had not paid her the slightest attention.
Unlikely as it seemed, that did not diminish her love.
She watched, applauded when he did well, and cried
for him when he did not. She read about his exploits
in the paper and eavesdropped shamelessly whenever
he was mentioned in passing conversations at balls.
He was the one of the few topics she would allow
Reggie to discuss in her presence. She pressed her
comrades to tell what they knew about him until they
bored of the subject. As she asked about many other
people as well, no one had ever noticed a particular
interest in the Marquis DeGuis.

She had, in fact, only confessed to her cousin Allison that she was in love, though she had refrained
from naming her hero. Margaret might lack tact, but
even she knew it was unthinkable to tell one's dearest
cousin that you are in love with the man she is about
to marry.

But he hadn't married Allison. She found that as
difficult to understand as everyone else. Certainly her
stepmother was baffled.

"Whistling her future down the wind!" Helen had
declared when they had received the letter from Som-
erset last autumn. "What can Allison be thinking?
The Marquis DeGuis is the catch of the Season—
handsome, refined, well-bred, and richer than Midas!
With Allison's looks and breeding, they would have
made such a handsome pair. Oh, your poor aunt
must be beside herself. Another Munroe sacrificed
to a country nobody!"

Margaret could not weep for her aunt or cousin.
At the reception, following the couple's elopement
to Gretna Green, Allison had appeared radiant be-

side her country nobody. No, Margaret had felt for the marquis, believing him to have lost his heart to her lovely cousin. Surely he was the one who was weeping.

She had been surprised, and a little disappointed, to find that he immediately reentered the lists when he returned to London after Christmas. As his own father had died at a young age, rumor had it he wanted to ensure the continuity of the line. After nearly two years of searching for a bride, he grew more impatient in setting up his nursery. The mamas with marriageable daughters mobbed him wherever he went.

Margaret stayed out of the way. She had little interest in being one of the pack, and she doubted he'd notice her even if she did join the hoards of ladies vying for his attentions. From his pursuit of first Allison and then Lady Janice, it appeared to Margaret that the Marquis DeGuis, like most of the gentlemen of the ton, was looking for the kind of wife he could display along with his trophies for fox hunting, boxing, and riding. Margaret Munroe refused to be anyone's trophy.

By May, it was clear that Lady Janice Willstencraft had gained the lead. That made it all the more difficult for Margaret, who had more than a passing acquaintance with Lady Janice. To have him court two of her friends was the outside of enough. Reggie told Margaret that betting at White's was heavily in favor of an engagement by June. Like so many others, Reggie had lost money on that wager, for here it was early July and Lady Janice was still not sporting a ring. Margaret wasn't sure why the marquis had waited, but she was certain it was only a matter of time. Lady Janice was beautiful—raven-haired, emerald-eyed, ivory-skinned. She was intelligent and spirited. She had the perfect flair to carry off the haughtiness required of a marchioness. The marquis would have his match at last. Reggie reported they were supposed to seal the deal within the week. The Marquis DeGuis would be forever beyond her reach, and she had never so much as danced with him.

In front of her, the dance had ended. The couples were regrouping for the next set. She could see no one she knew. She sagged in defeat. Much as she was tempted to accost a likely stranger and convince him to dance with her, she knew the deed would not go unpunished. Whether he agreed or not, someone would be sure to relay the tale to her stepmother. She wasn't sure the resulting scold was worth a dance, especially among so sedate a fellowship.

She sighed heavily and mentally consigned herself to surviving a boring evening until Reggie reappeared to take her home.

Behind her came the sound of a struggle. She turned in surprise and fell into a sturdy male body. Stumbling backward to apologize, she felt every ounce of blood drain from her body. Finding Reggie beaming at her, the whiff of alcohol tainting his breath, was bad enough. Seeing who she had collided with was much worse. The Marquis DeGuis looked anything but pleased by the event, handsome face positively scowling. She wondered if anyone would tell her stepmother if she simply bolted.

But it was too late for that.

"Cousin Margaret!" Reggie caroled as if he had been actually looking for her instead of avoiding her all evening. "I'm so pleased to find you."

Margaret took another step back from the powerful breath, but he reached out to snag her. Before she could pull away, she was thrust practically into the arms of the marquis, who actually cringed.

Please Lord, Margaret prayed. *Could I just die of mortification now?*

Her cousin by marriage had the audacity to turn his fatuous grin on her as she once more hastily separated herself from the marquis. "I was just telling my good friend the marquis how well you dance," he explained. "Be a dear, and partner him?"

Three

The poor woman stumbled back for the second time and stared at them, obviously aghast. Thomas inwardly cursed Pinstin's ineptitude. He shrugged him off at last and bowed to her. It was unthinkable to back out now. If she agreed, he would have to dance with her. As he straightened, she was still staring, and he offered her his best smile in hopes of putting her at her ease. Her pallor indicated she was stunned by Pinstin's precipitous suggestion, as would be any proper young lady of the ton. She was obviously a young lady of refinement, and her eccentricities were only a figment of Pinstin's drunken imagination and need to gossip. It would take all his tact to smooth over this gaff.

She blinked, collecting herself with obvious difficulty. "I'd be delighted, my lord," she murmured with a deeply respectful, and quite graceful, curtsy. He held out his arm, and she allowed him to lead her onto the floor. He cast a backward glare at Pinstin, but the fellow clasped both hands over his head in a sign of victory and grinned. Thomas wished him to perdition and took his place in the line across from Margaret.

It was a more sprightly dance than Thomas generally allowed himself. He usually did not appreciate

the weaving in and out and the promenading from
one end of the line of twenty couples to the other.
Most of his other partners made it into an endless
amount of tramping, all the while casting covert and
covetous glances at him over the tops of their ivory
and lace fans. Margaret Munroe, however, had obviously come to dance. After an initial hesitancy at being partnered with him, she quickly recovered. Her
blue eyes twinkled, she grinned at him whenever she
took his hands for the promenade, and when another
in their set swung her particularly well, she let forth
one of her marvelously unique laughs just for the joy
of it. Several of the other men around her smiled
along with Thomas. Several of the women scowled.

It was not until they stood out at the end of the
line for a round that he could really study her in
detail. As soon as Reggie had accosted her, he had
remembered her. He had been introduced to her at
a ball during the time he was courting Allison. Then,
he had paid her little heed, thinking himself already
settled in an engagement to her cousin. He had to
own, looking at her now, that he would probably have
paid her little heed even if he had been free then.
She would never have been his first choice in a bride.

While he did not insist on a particular look or coloring for his marchioness, he did have a vague notion
of what she would be like. She would be lovely, cul-
tured, calm, composed. She would carry herself like
a woman of good taste and breeding. She would be
able to command servants and entertain princes with
only a lifting of her eyebrow. Margaret Munroe fit
that image not in the slightest.

For one thing, she was entirely too animated. Allison's vivaciousness had been one of her most endearing traits. Margaret's boundless energy, on the
other hand, made him more than a little uncomfort-

able. He disliked being made a spectacle. Just being with the woman made him the target of inquisitive glances. He had wondered whether his sister might be considered colorless. Next to Margaret Munroe, he was the bland one.

For another thing, she was taller than any woman he had ever met. He had never been one to delight in the diminutive dolls who barely reached his chest. Neither did he feel particularly comfortable having a lady look him directly in the eye as Margaret was able to do, and rather appraisingly at that. Allison's eyes had been blue, if he remembered correctly, and he would be hard-pressed to forget Lady Janice's emerald gaze. Margaret's eyes, he saw, were a clear, pale blue that could sparkle like fine crystal in sunlight or cut through him like the blue steel of a rapier. The former look was present throughout most of the dance. The latter had been reserved for Pinstin, and he found himself hoping he was never the recipient.

For another matter, she was rather fierce-looking. Her nose was formidable, her lips generous. On the other hand, her figure was nothing short of impressive, and when all of it was in motion, as it had been when she was dancing, he found it hard not to appreciate the generous curves and graceful limbs. Perhaps her most striking feature, however, was her hair. It was thick and coarse, pulled up in a haphazard knot at the top of her head. What made it unusual was that at her young age the dusky black was already shot with gray, the color running through her tresses like veining in marble.

"Do you like the view?" she asked suddenly, and he jumped. "Yes, the gray is natural; the tendency runs in my family. No, I do not pad my chest. Is there anything else you'd like to know?"

Her comment should have been shocking, yet he

found himself licking his lips and managing a smile, feeling ill-mannered for the first time in his life. There was no doubt in his mind that she had uttered the comment solely for the purpose of making him feel foolish; but he found he could not bear her any ill will. That saucy grin was entirely too self-deprecating.

"Forgive my staring, Miss Munroe," he answered with a bow. "It has been a while since we last saw each other."

"At Lord Rillson's dinner party, last week, when you escorted Lady Janice Willstencraft," she replied readily, and now her eyes were definitely probing. "How is her ladyship by the way? Am I going to be called out for stealing you from her side?"

It was only the second time someone had asked him about the woman, but he felt himself stiffen. He told himself sternly he would have to get used to that sort of question. He had made his intentions toward Lady Janice abundantly clear. It was no wonder that people questioned when she did not appear on his arm. "Lady Janice Willstencraft is in no position to request my attentions," he told her, "now or in the future. She has chosen to pursue other entertainments."

"She was stupid enough to turn you down?" She frowned. "My opinion of the lady's intelligence has been significantly reduced."

He ought to protest, but the veiled compliment was balm to his wounded pride. In fact, as everyone assumed the ladies who had refused him were the idiots, he ought to feel entirely vindicated. Unfortunately, after a moment's thought, he only felt worse. All the denizens of the ton assumed he was as perfect as he appeared. Only the two ladies who had refused him knew otherwise. He was thankful that the dance required their attentions then, and he was spared having to respond to her.

It would have been easy to brood on his failures if it had not been for Miss Munroe's enthusiasm. Even if he did try not to look too often at those delightful limbs of hers, her laugh was impossible to ignore. If he was too slow in responding to the next movement, she captured his hands and pulled him along. If he lingered too long over his bow to the other lady in their set, she held out her hands imploringly, blue eyes crackling mischievously. He hadn't thought he was capable of smiling that evening, but by the time the dance ended his mouth seemed to be permanently fixed in that position. He bowed low to her.

"Miss Munroe, a delight. I don't know when I have enjoyed a dance more."

Instead of curtsying, she smiled and nodded. "You are a tolerable dancer, my lord. I suspect if you would relax a little, you would be a wonderful dancer."

He wasn't sure whether to be annoyed or amused. "Thank you, I think."

Her smile widened. "You're welcome, I'm quite sure. Are you willing to try another?"

If any other woman of his acquaintance had asked him, he would have thought her forward. Coming from Margaret Munroe, it seemed perfectly natural. However, two dances would have made a statement he was not prepared to make. It was well-known he had been courting Lady Janice until this very evening. To have switched his allegiance so swiftly to Miss Munroe, as dancing with her twice in a row would indicate, would surely set tongues wagging. They would wag enough it was known he had been rejected. He bowed again. "I regret that I have a previous engagement. Another time perhaps."

This time she did curtsy, but not before he saw

disappointment cut across her lovely eyes, like a cloud over a vibrant summer sky. "You are too kind, my lord," she murmured. Something in the tone made him go cold. It was as if she knew he was placating her. She knew he had been forced to dance with her. It must appear to her that he was making his escape as quickly as possible. He felt like a worm.

Rising, she offered him a parting smile, but this time it could only be called sad. "Do not look so troubled, my lord. You have not said or done anything that will cause the gossips to cackle. You're always the gentleman."

There was nothing in her tone that suggested a challenge, but he heard one nonetheless. Besides his failures in love, he had a single besetting sin. He simply could not ignore a challenge. The urge to excel had driven him into races that had nearly cost him his favorite horse. It had caused him to make a scene at a public assembly last year, a fact he wasn't sure he could ever forgive. It had also driven him to take on Allison's country squire in a bare knuckles brawl last autumn.

"Do you not appreciate gentlemen, Miss Munroe?" he asked, trying to still the familiar heating of his blood.

She cocked her head and narrowed her eyes. "Certainly, my lord. But I must admit that I prefer gentlemen who allow themselves to enjoy the moment."

"Ah, but one moment leads to the next," he chided her. "If we do not consider carefully, we may make decisions that will affect the rest of our lives."

She laughed her marvelous laugh. "Yes, and the ceiling may fall in the next minute and end our lives altogether. All there is is now, my lord. If you cannot find pleasure in it, you are not alive at all."

The philosophy was so foreign to him that he stood

frowning at her. The idea seemed entirely too sim-
plistic to him. How could one possibly enjoy the moment when there were estates to be managed, sisters
to be married off, a country to run? Was it truly possible to focus all one's energies, for a single moment,
on a single person or activity? The thought repelled
and intrigued him. However, thirty-two years of polished restraint were simply not broken in one moment's consideration. The couples moved around
them. At the top of the room, the musicians tuned
up for a waltz. Behind him, Margaret scowled suddenly.

"And here is my moment," she proclaimed. "And
I shall have to be content to watch. They're playing
a waltz and I haven't a partner."

He stiffened. He could not waltz; he'd never
learned. Frankly when the dance had begun to become popular last Season, he had thought it improper in the extreme. Such closeness was best
reserved for private moments. He had been surprised
to hear that the visiting Russian Czar had recently
gone so far as to dance it at Almack's, that infamous
ladies' club. He had never waltzed with Allison or
Lady Janice. Now he had a sudden image of Miss
Munroe's curves in his arms as he swirled her about
the dance floor and felt as if his face were flaming.
It must have been the refusal that made him think
such wild thoughts. He should take himself home
before he made a fool of himself.

He bowed to her again. "I regret, Miss Munroe,
that I do not waltz. Though if I did, I cannot imagine
a more delightful partner."

Her smile was dazzling. "But I would be happy to
teach you, my lord, if you're willing to try with such
an audience."

He wasn't willing in the slightest. He shook his

head. "Thank you, but no. I'd better retire while I still can." He started to turn, and suddenly it seemed as if everyone in the ballroom had frozen. Across the dance floor, Lady Janice had returned. His gaze met hers. That those emerald eyes were red-rimmed, as if she had just finished a prolonged bout of crying, should have made him feel better. All he felt was guilt. He glanced quickly at Miss Munroe, then back at Lady Janice, whose eyes had narrowed, making her look decidedly feline.

"You can't leave now," Margaret said quietly beside him. "She'll think you're running away."

Thomas frowned. "I have never run from anything in my life."

"Then don't start now," she advised. "If you won't waltz, perhaps a promenade? Standing there glaring at her will not help matters, you know."

"I do not glare," he said, glaring at her. She smiled sweetly, and he felt his anger melting. He chuckled, offering her his arm. "Very well, Miss Munroe. A few more minutes will not matter. Let us promenade."

They walked up and down the narrow room for a time, neither saying anything. Thomas took several deep breaths and forced his mind to clear. While he had found Lady Janice composed and queenly, in truth he had never felt an undying passion for her. Certainly he had never been as fond of her as he had been of Allison. Thinking on it now, he realized that it had been the attack, which had so mirrored the heart failure that had taken his father, that had driven him to find another candidate for his bride so quickly, and not some fascination with Lady Janice's charms. There was no reason for him to be uncomfortable near her. No reason except the fact that she knew he had failed.

"You could probably apologize," Margaret murmured beside him. "Or get her to. If you love each other, that is."

Again she was being impertinent. His feelings toward Lady Janice, or lack thereof, were his own business. Yet she offered the suggestion as from one good friend to another. Even if she hadn't, he would have judged the advice sound.

"Thank you for your concern, my dear," he replied, "but I think it safe to say that both Lady Janice and I are agreed to the end of our courtship."

"It's not like you to give up without a fight," she protested. "You were passionate in your defense of Wellington's budget and the proper provisioning of our troops in France. You tried valiantly to turn the tide of sentiment against Leigh Hunt when he was on trial for using the press to report on the reprehensible doings of the Prince."

He frowned, gazing at her. "How do you know that?"

She colored, the red in her cheeks clashing with the fluffy pink dress. "It was in the *Times,*" she murmured defensively.

He added a healthy interest in politics to her growing list of admirable qualities. Pinstin's words struck him again. Could it be that he had been letting a pretty face and a composed manner dictate his choice of bride?

"Then I cannot convince you to reconcile?" she pressed him.

And selfless as well, Thomas thought, wondering how many other young ladies of the ton would have thought of his happiness rather than their chances of taking Lady Janice's place in his affections. Her unlooked for devotion was so kind, he brought her hand to his lips and kissed it. The redoubtable Miss

Munroe stumbled and he had to help her back onto her feet.

"Sorry," she mumbled, swallowing convulsively. "Must have been a bump in the carpet." Thomas looked away to give her a moment to compose herself, marveling that so small a matter as a kiss on the hand could be so disturbing. He had used the gesture any number of times with other ladies to show appreciation. Certainly his other kisses did not engender such a response. He pushed the painful thought away. That's when he noticed the number of people staring at them. Across the room, Pinstin grinned conspiratorially at him.

Thomas frowned. Even without a second dance it seemed the ton thought he had shifted his affections. The rumors would do his reputation, and Miss Munroe's, little good.

She must have seen the stares as well for she gave his arm a reassuring squeeze. "Do not let them trouble you, my lord. None of them would seriously believe you are courting me. I'm an Original. You have much more refined taste than to hook yourself up to one of those."

Refined taste he might have, but it had not gotten him his marchioness. The young lady on his arm had already showed herself to have more appreciation and understanding than either of the young ladies he had previously chosen to court. He knew he wasn't ready for another courtship, but he could not allow the gossips to say he had been using Miss Munroe, as would undoubtedly happen if he did not further their acquaintance. He stopped their walk and bowed to her.

"You underestimate yourself, madame," he told her truthfully. "I find myself intrigued. Are you free next Friday, around three?"

She was staring again, but this time she appeared to be in shock. "Yes, certainly, whatever time is convenient," she stammered.

"Until then," he replied with a bow. As he turned to leave, he told himself he ought to be depressed. He'd been turned down again and had precipitously decided to investigate a woman who could only be called unique. Yet he felt absurdly pleased with himself. Perhaps there was something to this living in the moment.

Four

"The Marquis DeGuis!" her stepmother cried, staring at Reggie as if he'd lost his mind. "The Marquis DeGuis is coming to call? On Margaret?"

"You're teasing us, boy," her father maintained. "Everyone knows he's set his cap for the Willstencraft girl."

Margaret glared at her cousin's gloating face as he sat across from them in the family sitting room of their London townhouse. She had fully intended to keep the matter quiet as long as possible, but here it was only the day after the ball and Reggie, who couldn't have been bothered to pay attention to her for most of the evening, could scarcely contain himself another moment.

"I assure you, she is the talk of the ton!" he declared, fanning himself as if the stories were simply too heated to bear. "She has eclipsed even the tales of the visiting Russian court, not to mention Kean's popularity at the theater! I had no idea when I introduced Margaret to the marquis that his interest would last above a moment. For my little cousin to have attracted someone like DeGuis, well, all I can say is that I am in awe."

Margaret stood up to remind him that his little cousin could fully look him in the eye should he be man enough to stand. "If you cannot make better conversation than that," she advised him, "you may leave right now."

"Margaret, please!" her stepmother commanded, plying her hands in equal agitation. "I simply do not understand this. The Marquis DeGuis is coming to call on you?"

"As he didn't ask after you or Father," Margaret replied tartly, "I can only assume he's coming to call on me." When Mrs. Munroe sputtered incoherently and her father blinked in confusion, she decided she had been right in wanting to wait to tell them. Their amazement was amusing, until one stopped to consider its source. Then her own composure was shaken. Deep down, she also found it unlikely that the marquis might want to further his acquaintance.

Reggie was equally amazed. "It is hard to credit, Aunt Helen, I agree. After Uncle Marcus's cousin Allison and Lady Janice, who would have thought the marquis would settle for someone like our Margaret?"

"She's a clever gel," her father put in loyally. "Haven't I always said so?"

"Clever, certainly," her stepmother allowed. "But to catch a man like the marquis? I agree with Reggie. I simply cannot credit it."

"I haven't caught him," Margaret pointed out. "He is only coming to call."

"And why should he do that if he is not interested?" Helen demanded. She eyed Reggie speculatively. "What else do you know, nephew? Are they placing bets at White's?"

"Probably," Mr. Munroe muttered. "Seems they bet on most anything these days."

"In truth I have not had an opportunity to check," Reggie replied, preening that he had their full attention. "I came here straight away to congratulate my cousin."

"If you'd paid attention, you could have congratulated me last night," Margaret pointed out. "And spared me this humiliation."

Reggie spread his hands. "But if I'd been too attentive, you might never have had the opportunity to attach him. Are you not pleased I led him to you?"

"No more arguing," her stepmother declared. "We have too much to do." She clasped her long-fingered hands together reverently, button-brown eyes gleaming with matronly delight. "The Marquis DeGuis! And to think you took him right out from under Lady Janice Willstencraft's nose."

Margaret refrained from explaining that he had been more thrust into her lap than taken away. She refused to spread gossip. The poor man had been through enough. Two refusals in less than a year would dampen the ardor of the most romantic of gentlemen. She had seen the hurt in his eyes last night when he had watched Lady Janice return to the ballroom. She had also seen the frustration in the other young lady's eyes when she had seen Margaret with the marquis. If Lady Janice could be jealous of so unlikely a rival as Margaret, she obviously still carried some strong feelings for the marquis. Despite the marquis' denial, they would no doubt soon reconcile.

She said as much. Mrs. Munroe looked horrified.

"Think shame on yourself for wishing this opportunity away," she scolded. "For once in your life, Margaret, have some care for the future. Reggie, it was most kind of you to come tell us the news, especially as Margaret did not see fit to do so. I must ask you to leave us, now. We have much to accomplish."

For once, Reggie did not attempt to prolong the visit. He rose eagerly, no doubt, Margaret thought, to spread his gossip to all who would listen. She was sure he would make the most of the upcoming visit, as for once he would appear the hero of the tale.

"You should not get your hopes up," Margaret told her stepmother as soon as Reggie was safely out the door. "I am sincerely grateful that I actually got a dance out of the Marquis DeGuis. But he is only coming Friday out of a sense of duty. There can be no other explanation."

"I *will* get my hopes up," Mrs. Munroe countered. "You have a chance, Margaret, and it is my duty as your father's wife to make sure you make the most of it. Marcus, I expect you to loosen the purse strings. She needs an entire new wardrobe, and we must refurbish the withdrawing room, by Friday."

That set her father to arguing. Margaret watched their good-natured bickering for a moment. Her stepmother always reminded her of a militant rabbit, with her bright eyes tucked deep in a round, soft-skinned face. She was shorter than Margaret by over a head, and outweighed her by over three stone. As her own mother had died when Margaret was seven, she had little with which to compare her stepmother. From stories her father told, Margaret thought the only things she had inherited from her mother were the woman's strength of will, her graceful movements, and her impressive bustline.

Margaret did not have to look at her father to be reminded what he looked like. Everything she had not inherited from her mother—formidable nose, generous mouth, piercing blue eyes, towering height—she had inherited from her father. At fifty-five, he was completely gray, his coarse hair flying at all angles about his long face. A second son of a second son, he had had to earn a living as a secretary to a venerable military man early in his life. Some well-placed investments in the Exchange had netted him enough to remarry a widow of some social standing, retire into gentile poverty, and pretend he was every bit as refined as his wealthier Munroe cousins. Now he spent his days reading and debating with others of his rank in the various gentlemen's clubs, with an occasional evening's entertainment organized by this capable wife. She caught herself wondering how soon the marquis might be invited to one of her stepmother's fetes and shook her head. The marquis was not likely to be in her life long enough for him to so much as take tea. She would assuage his sense of propriety by going through with the visit. She was certain he would not be calling again.

Her father was showing signs of weakness, edging out of the wing-backed chair as if he wanted to escape the decision. Her stepmother was using the unethical weapons of family loyalty and love for his daughter, arguments her poor father would have a difficult time countering. Margaret reentered the fray.

"I have no interest in a new dress, and we have no time to reupholster the furniture," she pointed out. "Even if we had the money to do so."

"There, you see?" her father caroled, seizing the lifeline. "She's quite right. The marquis was interested in Margaret, after all. I doubt he will so much as glance at the furnishings."

"That's how much you know," Helen replied with a sniff. "We must make the best impression. But you are correct that time is short. We will simply have to use the withdrawing room."

Her father looked impressed. The last time the room had been used was for the reception following the death of his father, some four years ago. The furniture there was elegant with scrolled backs and arms of polished wood and muted patterns of gold on navy. It was also stiff from lack of use. One could not slouch in the withdrawing room. One could only sit ramrod straight.

But if her father thought that assigning the visit to the little used room would be simple, he was doomed to disappointment. It seemed everything on the ground floor of the little house had to be inspected, repaired, and cleaned, even if the marquis was unlikely to so much as set foot in any room but the withdrawing room.

"We cannot be certain he will not notice other rooms," her stepmother replied when Margaret pointed out the illogic. "First impressions are vital, Margaret. I will not have him think you out of fashion."

"But we are out of fashion," Margaret tried, helping their diminutive maid Becky shove a sofa off the carpet so it could be cleaned. "Couldn't we just admit that and save ourselves considerable work?"

Becky brightened, but Mrs. Munroe's frown was sufficiently quelling that neither of them dared broach the subject again.

With only the maid and their cook to help, the work took much of the few days remaining. Unfortunately, it was not sufficiently challenging work that it kept Margaret from brooding. Forced nearly every minute to prepare for the visit, she could hardly keep from thinking about it. It also did not help that Reggie popped in from time to time to report the ton's perception of this visit. Bets at White's were running heavily in favor of a reconciliation with Lady Janice. Reggie even went so far as to imply that the visit was merely an attempt at revenge against the lady. Mar-

garet laughed even as her stepmother looked horrified.

"I'm a poor choice to make the lady jealous," she
told them. Then she sobered, remembering the look
in the lady's eyes the last time she had seen her. Still,
she could not believe the marquis would be so petty.
Much as she supported mending one's heart after a
painful romantic interlude, revenge seemed a paltry
way to go about it. She'd recommend a ten-mile ride,
a warm bath, and a good book, in that order. And
perhaps a retreat to the country for a few weeks. She
had heard he had a lovely retreat in the Lake District,
which would surely be the ticket. Certainly such a
remedy would be more useful than pretending to
court her.

By Friday morning, Mrs. Munroe declared the
house suitable for the marquis' visit. The formal withdrawing room had been aired, dusted, polished, and
fluffed. The marble tiles in the little entryway
gleamed. The banister on the stairs to the second
floor was warm in its thick polish. With the house in
order, however, her stepmother's attentions immediately shifted to Margaret, towing her upstairs to consider her wardrobe and coiffure. She sank onto the
stool before her cluttered dressing table and steeled
herself for the onslaught. Mrs. Munroe immediately
started questioning her choice of dress, preferring
an insipid yellow ruffled sarcenet to the simple white
sprigged muslin Margaret refused to take off. She
then insisted on styling Margaret's hair in sausage-
shaped curls on either side of her long face, which,
to Margaret's opinion, merely called attention to her
nose. And worst of all, she kept up a constant stream
of instructions as she did so.

"Remember not to talk unless he speaks first. We
want him to think you demure."

"Too late for that," Margaret declared, but Helen only frowned at her before continuing.

"Laugh at his quips. Men like that. But please don't laugh like you usually do. A lady-like giggle will suffice. Try to remember you are not a gentleman."

Margaret bit back a laugh that would only have distressed her stepmother. "I doubt I'll consider myself a gentleman while the marquis is here," she managed with a relatively straight face.

Her stepmother seemed to be satisfied with that, hurrying from the room to make sure all was in readiness for the visit. As soon as she was gone, Margaret combed her hair out and tucked it up on top of her head.

Shortly before three, all was ready. Mrs. Munroe confined Margaret to her room with the admonition not to muss herself. Margaret sat on the bed, then rose, concerned she might further wrinkle the muslin. She paced instead, then jumped when Becky knocked to tell her she could come down. She swallowed the lump of nervousness in her throat and hurried after her.

The marquis was already sitting properly in one of the armchairs when she arrived. He was probably the only person in the world who could look comfortable and in command in the stiff chairs. He was arrayed in a splendid coat of camel-colored superfine and tan chamois trousers tucked into gleaming Hessians. He rose as she entered, and she did not think it was her imagination that he looked relieved to see her. She wondered what her stepmother had been saying to him. Mrs. Munroe was glowing possessively. Margaret and the marquis had no more than greeted each other and seated themselves before Mrs. Munroe made the flimsiest of excuses and quit the room with a knowing glance at Margaret. She was giving the marquis a moment to propose. The idea was so ludicrous that Margaret's nervousness evaporated in amusement.

"I'm now supposed to captivate you with my stimulating conversation," she informed him in the silence that followed her stepmother's precipitous departure. "As we both know this visit is a sham, perhaps we could just dispense with the formalities."

He frowned. "I'm not sure what you mean by sham, Miss Munroe. Are you under the impression that my intentions are less than honorable?"

Having both heard of and been witness to his proper lifestyle, she could not help but chuckle. "Oh, no, my lord. I'm sure your intentions, if you had any, would be entirely honorable. I simply thought it best that we be honest with each other from the beginning and acknowledge the fact that you are here only because of Lady Janice."

He rose and walked to the window, but not fast enough to hide the fact that he had paled. "Have the rumors spread so quickly?"

"I have no doubt the gossip is flying," she replied, refraining from mentioning her cousin's stream of it. "But I was there at the ball, remember?"

She thought his shoulders sagged in his relief and wondered suddenly whether there was more to the story of Lady Janice's refusal than she had thought. If he did stay in her life long enough, she might have to have a talk with the lady. Surely Lady Janice would tell her the truth of the matter.

"You are very good at being forthright," he said to the window.

"Painfully so," she acknowledged cheerfully. "And I do expect the same of others. So, out with it, my lord. You are only here to prove to society that you were not trifling with my affections. Let us have a

decent conversation and set you free from this onerous duty." She knew the words sounded like a challenge and steeled herself for his concurrence. He
stiffened as if making some resolution then strode
back to her side. Sitting beside her on the sofa, he
took her hands in his. Margaret looked up in surprise
at the intensity of his gaze.

"Miss Munroe, you must believe me. I would not
be here if I were not sincere in my admiration of
you."

She would have given anything to hear that speech
and believe it. She snatched her hands away from
him, leaning back against the opposite arm of the
sofa to put distance between them. "Rubbish! Do you
think me so feather-brained? You have not spent
more than a half hour in my company since the day
we met over a year ago. During that time, you sincerely courted two other women. You cannot admire
me. You don't even know me."

He swallowed, lowering his gaze. "You are right, of
course. I did not mean to imply that I had formed
an attachment in so short a time. That would be quite
unseemly."

Though she had known the truth, his statement
still hurt, for her own attachment had been formed
quickly and surely. "Not unseemly, my lord. Just unlikely."

"Agreed. I know very little about you, as you noted.
However, I must insist that what I know is wholly admirable. You are sharp-witted; you seem to have a joy
of life I have seen in few others; and your laugh is
altogether delightful."

"Really?" she squeaked, then swallowed the
astonishment and pleasure that was preventing co-
herent thought, much less speech.

"Really." He smiled. The smile lit his eyes with blue

flame, like brandy around a plum pudding. It both warmed and thrilled her.

"I will not claim to be courting," he continued, "but I see no harm in a friendship. Will you allow me the opportunity to get to know you better?"

She could only nod, overcome by the tumult of emotions. She could not have attracted his attentions. A friendship was more than she had thought possible, yet how insipid it seemed. Her cousin Allison had inspired an offer of marriage after only a few encounters, and the best Margaret could do was a friendship? The second-rate Munroes were a dismal second this time. Yet even as she sighed, she felt a tingle of hope. Stranger things than friendship had led to romance.

He continued to smile at her and her heart turned over. "Perhaps we might go driving tomorrow?" he asked.

She knew this was one of those times when she should do as her stepmother suggested and simply agree. Yet she had told him she wanted to be honest "I abhor driving in the city traffic, my lord," she confessed. "Could we not ride in the park?"

His smile deepened. "That would be delightful. Shall I call for you at this time tomorrow?"

She didn't want to be difficult. But riding in the park at three was simply not riding at all. "If one is really to ride, my lord, you will have to start earlier than that. I generally take Aeolus out at eight each morning."

"Then I shall be pleased to join you," he replied, but his smile was beginning to look strained. He rose and offered her a bow. "And now, I had best be on my way before I overstay my welcome."

"You could never do that," she told him, but she rose and curtsied. "Allow me to show you out."

He did not protest as she led him down the corridor to the small entryway, where his hat and cane lay waiting as she had thought they might across the half-moon table against the wall.

He accepted them, turning the brim of the hat around in his hands before donning it. "Thank you for seeing me out, Miss Munroe. It was most gracious of you."

"Not at all," Margaret replied with a smile. "You must understand that there is method in my madness. The moment you leave, my stepmother will interrogate me endlessly. I'm only seeking to hold her off as long as possible."

He glanced over his shoulder and there was the unmistakable sound of a door closing somewhere behind them. He looked back at Margaret and winked. Her heart sang.

"In that case, I regret I did not stay longer. You may assure Mrs. Munroe that I found the visit delightful." He raised her hand to his lips and brushed them across the back. Then, tipping his hat, he walked out the door.

Margaret shut the door and leaned against it, staring unseeing at the corridor. She ought to be similarly delighted, but she only felt a rising panic. The man she adored most in all the world, a man who was totally unsuited to her personally, wanted to further the acquaintance.

What was she to do now?

Five

What was he to do now?

The rather companionable feelings he had shared with Margaret in the entryway vanished almost immediately as he climbed into his carriage. In truth, when he had left home, he was determined not to call again after today. Her stepmother's reception, with that salivating look he had seen so often since he declared he was on the marriage mart, had only reinforced his opinion. He shouldn't be courting anyone just yet. He needed time to survey the prospects, discuss the matter over dinner with a few choice friends, consider what had gone wrong the first two times, and determine how to fix it. That last activity should not take much time. He was fairly confident he knew what had ruined his chances with Allison and Lady Janice. He would not be so precipitous the next time.

But then Margaret Munroe had entered the room with a glow in her eyes that told him how sincerely glad she was to see him. When she had accused him, rather correctly, of false intentions, he found he could not use her so ill. She did have traits that might be good in a marchioness—intelligence, honesty, what appeared to be loyalty. Perhaps, if he got to know her better, he would find that she might suit after all.

Still, he wasn't entirely sure how to proceed with something that was not yet a courtship. He could not remember ever feeling at such a loss in either of his other pursuits. He had quickly determined that Allison and Lady Janice had the stuff for a marchioness and made his intentions plain to the parents of his chosen bride, long before he had made them clear to either of them. There had been several well-chosen, properly chaperoned appearances in public—balls, the opera, a drive through Hyde Park. While Allison had asked some difficult questions and Lady Janice had been demanding of his attention, neither had made him search his motives, his actions, or his very character. Margaret Munroe had a way of looking at him that made him acutely aware that he had other failings than the one that had made Allison and Lady Janice refuse him.

Yet he could not hide away from what she made him see. He liked to think he was an honorable man, and a truthful one. If there was something in him that compromised that honor, it must be excised. He may not have started this acquaintance with her with the best of intentions, but he would proceed with them. Besides, he felt more alive now than after any of the dances or visits to either of his other ladies. Perhaps it was time he approached courtship differently. A friendship might be a good start, and it would be far less taxing to his emotions.

He hated to admit it, but after two tries, he was beginning to feel a trifle bruised. He had done his best to convince Allison he was worthy of her hand, yet she had turned from him to an oafish brute of a country squire. He had been more cautious with Lady Janice, yet still she refused him. This time, he would go even more slowly and guard his heart. If there was any rejecting to be done, he would be the one to do so. Miss Margaret Munroe was not getting under his skin. He simply would not allow it.

Of course, a lot was going to depend on the lady herself. She was right that he actually knew only a little about her. It seemed to him Allison had mentioned her on more than one occasion, but he could not recall the content of the discussion. There was of course the nonsense Pinstin had mouthed at the ball, but he did not put much faith in the truth of it. Gossip was for fools and cowards. Surely the best way to know the lady was to spend considerable time in her company. He would start tomorrow.

He generally rose at nine in town, had a simple breakfast, and attended to his estate business before joining his peers in Parliament in the afternoon. When he rode, it was generally before changing for dinner. The morning he was to go riding with Margaret, he woke at seven. From that moment, nothing went right. His bleary-eyed valet, Jimms, who had never done anything the least offensive, actually nicked him while shaving him, forcing him to change his shirt.

"Sorry, my lord," the poor fellow apologized, "my hands are simply not steady this early in the morning." The valet managed to find some sticking plaster to staunch the tiny drips of blood, and Thomas changed into his navy riding coat and cream trousers and went to breakfast with the white plaster pointing like a finger out of his chin.

Cook had his habitual tea and toast ready, but one sip of the tea easily burned his mouth.

"Sorry, my lord," the footman demurred, hastily removing the steaming cup. "It usually has more time to cool before you arrive."

The groomsman was just checking his saddle when he strode down from the house to his horse. He had to wait until all the girths had been properly cinched.

"Sorry, my lord," the man murmured, stepping away so Thomas could mount.

"Don't tell me," Thomas snapped. "The horses aren't used to getting up this early either."

"They may be," the fellow grinned saucily, "but the rest of us aren't." He ducked his head and hurried away from Thomas' answering glare.

Am I such a creature of habit? Thomas wondered as he set off for Margaret's on the edge of Mayfair. He had never considered himself wedded to a particular schedule, but this morning certainly indicated he had fallen into a calculated rut. While there was a certain comfort in routine, he didn't want to become a slave to it. He chucked to the Arabian and cantered down the street so that he might still arrive before eight.

There was a spirited thoroughbred gelding waiting impatiently in the street in front of the Munroe house, a powerful black beast nearly seventeen hands high. He looked as if he should be dragging a cannon into battle. His dun gelding Nicodemus snorted and skitted aside when the other horse tossed its head and whinnied in challenge. Annoyed that he would have to share the ride with another gentleman, for surely only a man would ride such an animal, he jumped from the saddle. Tossing the reins to the mews boy who stood waiting, he climbed the stairs to the townhouse door.

It opened before he could knock. Margaret Munroe offered him a cheerful smile and ran lightly down the stairs to the waiting horse. She patted the beast in welcome, and it whickered in recognition. The boy holding her reins grinned at her.

"Coming, my lord?" she called, picking up the skirt of her cobalt velvet riding habit to climb the mounting block.

Thomas shook himself and hurried to join her.

"You intend to ride this beast?" he asked with a slight frown, noticing the side saddle for the first time. Though the horse seemed easy with her, he wasn't sure he could be easy with her up on such an animal.

"Certainly." Margaret smiled at him. "I've ridden Aeolus every morning for four years." She glanced at his Arabian, who somehow looked small and dainty next to the black. "Though I appreciate the lines of that fellow. Shall we be off?"

Thomas managed a returning smile, still wary, and held out a hand to help her. She either didn't notice or ignored him, hitching herself up into the side saddle as if from long practice. Shaking his head, he climbed into his own saddle and drew his horse abreast of hers. The black mouthed the bit as if he wanted to turn and nip the Arabian, but Margaret held him steady. With a twinkle in her eyes that promised fun, she urged the horse forward and they started for the park.

"A lovely morning for a ride," he ventured, attempting to put the situation back onto a more traditional footing.

As if to disagree, she eyed the chimneys of the houses they passed, where smoke from morning fires obscured the blue of the sky. Funny how he'd never noticed that before.

"I hope this wasn't too early for you," she replied.

He started to demur, but his conscience nagged him. She was endlessly honest; she had said she expected the same from him. "Eight was earlier than I had thought," he allowed, touching his cut chin. The plaster bumped his finger and he snatched it off, trying not to color.

She gave her signature laugh, and he had to join her. "Next time," she promised, "we'll go when you choose."

The idea that there would be a next time somehow pleased him and the pleasure surprised him. They rode on in companionable silence until they reached the park.

Thomas was further surprised to find that there were quite a few people up and moving at so unfashionable an hour. Several couples strolled the paths and more horses trotted along the riding trails. Still, it was far less crowded than in the afternoon when he usually rode. He found himself enjoying the openness.

And he found himself enjoying the company. She asked no more probing questions, discussing the races he had entered as if she had seen them.

"I'm not sure which I enjoy more," she confided when he tried a question of his own, regarding her preference for horse or carriage racing. "Horse racing is thrilling—just the rider and his mount pitted against the hordes. But with carriage racing, you must be more cunning. There are the added dimensions of the vehicle, its weight and design and wheel circumference that one must consider."

"Very wise," Thomas allowed, hiding his surprise that she should have thought about such issues. "I had not thought about it, but you are right that in carriage racing, one is at the mercy of the carriage maker. If there is a flaw in the wood of the yoke or if the wheel was not bent properly, you have lost."

"We agree," she replied with a smile as if that were an amazing thing. "In horse racing, you have only to worry about two flaws—yours and the horse's."

"And what flaws does this fellow have?" Thomas nodded to the thoroughbred, who rolled his eye as if he knew he were under discussion.

"Aeolus, my king of the winds?" She smiled fondly. "He is stubborn and irascible, not unlike his owner. But he makes up his mind about people and situations quickly, and you cannot sway him with sweet words."

"I am doomed," Thomas predicted.

She laughed. After she sobered, he caught her eyeing him speculatively. "And your mount, my lord? It's hard to imagine so graceful an animal having flaws."

He patted the dun's neck. The horse picked up his pace a little. "Nicodemus is perhaps overly fastidious. He is swift to run, but he likes his way to be predictable. A new statue or plant along the path will deter him as if he thinks it inappropriate."

"And his master?" she teased. "Has he any hidden flaws?"

He wanted to answer with a quip, but his recent refusal was too much on his mind. "They are too numerous to list," he replied with a sigh.

She chuckled. "You are doing it entirely too brown. Only you would think yourself flawed. Perfection often cannot recognize itself."

He could feel himself coloring and she clucked to the black, riding a little way ahead as if to give him a moment to compose himself. A DeGuis, needing to recover his composure, in the middle of Hyde Park. He was clearly overwrought. Shaking his head, he nudged the dun back to her side along the flower-bordered path.

They had reached Hyde Park corner, lorries and wagons trundling past just outside the enclosing fence. Beside them began Rotten Row. The sandy riding track stretched invitingly into the distance. Another time, he would have loved to see how fast he could take it. With present company, of course, it was unthinkable. While Allison had begged him to ride with her there, he had always refused. Ladies did not ride on Rotten Row.

"Race you to the Serpentine, my lord?" Margaret grinned.

He smiled. "A bold jest, my dear. Much as I enjoy The Row, I quite prefer present company."

Her grin faded to be replaced by a frown. "I wasn't joking. Aeolus and I have taken Rotten Row any number of times. I was inviting you to race with us."

Pinstin had claimed she was a bruising rider but Thomas had not believed him. It struck him now that her points on racing had been grounded on practice, not philosophy. He could not seem to still his disapproval. "Don't be ridiculous. Women shouldn't race."

"Anyone who rides a horse well and enjoys the sport should race," she countered. "And while I dislike bragging, I have to admit I ride quite well. You've just finished telling me how well you ride. The path lies open. Let's race."

He could feel the desire building inside him to do just that. The vision of her flying along beside him made his face crack in a grin. Her eyes lighted as well. He forced himself to frown. "Miss Munroe, if you have no care for your own safety, I must. I cannot race with you."

"If I were a man you'd race with me," she accused.

"If you were a man," Thomas snapped, "I wouldn't be out riding with you at this ungodly hour!"

She glared at him. "So sorry to have inconvenienced you, my lord. I assure you it won't happen again. Pray do not let us detain you." She tightened her grip on the reins and pressed her heels into the flanks of the black. Aeolus flattened his ears and broke into a gallop onto The Row.

Thomas gritted his teeth. He counted to ten. He scolded himself for his lack of willpower. The challenge of her quickly disappearing back mocked him. He pressed the Arabian into a gallop and tore off after her.

She was not easy to catch. The massive thoroughbred started slowly, but he gained speed with each stretch of his powerful legs. It was perhaps five hundred yards to where the path opened onto the Serpentine. She had already crossed fifty yards of the distance when he started forward with Nicodemus. He crouched low over the dun's neck, urging the beast to a faster pace even as his blood heated with the familiar tang of competition. The lighter Arabian sprinted easily. Trees shot by on either side. People strolling on the paths that paralleled The Row stopped to watch him. A silver-haired matron raised her quizzing glass. Another gentleman rider heard the thunder of his hooves and pulled aside to let him pass. Ahead of him, through a haze of dust, he saw Margaret.

She glanced back at him and bent forward herself. Her laughter floated to him in challenge. The minx was thoroughly enjoying herself! Grinning, Thomas urged his horse faster.

They pelted down the stretch of the path, Thomas's mount edging closer with each moment. The black swerved away from the encroaching dun, and Thomas pressed into the gap. Margaret cast him a quick look, eyes alight, grinning with joy. They shot past the overlook to the Serpentine together. Thomas pulled into the lead just before they were forced to slow for a group of riders ahead of them.

"Well done," she cried, pulling abreast. "Thank you for an exciting diversion, my lord."

He couldn't help but return her smile. His blood was singing in his veins, the air tasted sweet, and he hadn't felt so alive in a very long time. "You are quite welcome, Miss Munroe. I begin to see what you mean about living in the moment."

"I thought you might," she replied with a nod. "We'll have to see that you enjoy yourself more often."

Her eyes were bluer than the sky above them; her lips pinker than the roses in the nearby gardens. He had a sudden desire to feel those lips against his own. The idea was so improper and dangerous that he nearly dropped the reins. The responsive dun faltered in his paces.

"I think perhaps Nicodemus has had enough for one day," he said to hide the gaff. "Perhaps we should head for home."

She looked disappointed, but nodded again and continued along beside him. As they rode out of the park, he wondered whether he was fooling anyone. There simply was no way to deny that Margaret Munroe had a unique way of cutting up his peace. This friendship might prove more dangerous than he had thought.

Six

Having reached the safety of her room by the back stair without encountering her stepmother, Margaret shrugged out of her riding habit. She felt as if her body glowed with pleasure. From the first time she had met Thomas, she had felt he embodied all that was right in a man. He was noble, kind, courageous, and intelligent. Of course, no one was entirely perfect. A handsome profile, stunning physique, sharp wit, and gentlemanly bearing were nothing without an impassioned heart. She had considered his courtship of her cousin restrained, but she had thought he was surely more effusive in private. When Allison had rejected him, she had wept for him. When Lady Janice had refused him, she had wanted to scratch her eyes out. When he had turned so quickly to Margaret, she had begun to fear that her perfect man had a heart of clay.

After the race today, however, and the desire that had flamed briefly in his sapphire eyes, she knew otherwise. There was a passion inside him to match all his other wonderful attributes. She had only to find a way for him to share it with her.

She still could not believe she had much of a chance. She was not ashamed of her standing in the ton, but she was not blind to it either. A perfect fellow like the marquis would have trouble explaining his interest in a woman like Margaret. However, much as she yearned to be his bride, she had never allowed her life to be dictated by the whims of fashion; she wasn't about to change that now.

Her stepmother, of course, was another story. "What happened?" she demanded when Margaret appeared downstairs at last. "Why didn't you come to me straight off? I was watching the window. I didn't even see you return."

"We returned through the mews," Margaret explained, taking a seat beside her in the worn family sitting room. It still bore the signs of recent cleaning, the scratched and dented furniture gleaming in the light of the twin windows. She gave her stepmother a sketchy account of the ride, but, as expected, when she came to the part about the race, Mrs. Munroe stopped her.

"Oh, Margaret, you didn't!" she moaned. "How many times have I warned you! It is bad enough to race about the country when we are visiting your cousins. Few people will see you and they are not of consequence. How could you do something so reprehensible in front of the marquis of all people!"

"Racing is not reprehensible," Margaret replied, thoroughly glad her father had not repeated the tales of her London races to her stepmother. "A number of people do it, even women."

"Women," Mrs. Munroe sniffed, "not ladies."

"Yes, even ladies. In any event, it was early. There were few people about so we did not encounter anyone we know. I doubt it will be remarked upon."

"And for that you may be thankful. However, the primary question is this: have you damaged your chances with the marquis? How did he react to this race?"

Remembering the fire in his eyes when they had finished, Margaret smiled. "I think he was rather pleased by the turn of events."

Mrs. Munroe clapped her hands. "Clever girl! Hasn't your father always said so? When is he calling again?"

Margaret's smile faded. "He didn't say."

"What?" Her stepmother's eyes widened. "Oh, I knew it! You have frightened him away! We must find a way to make amends. Perhaps you can send him a note. No, that would be unseemly. Perhaps we can have a party and invite him."

"You know we cannot afford that so soon after your dinner party last week," Margaret reminded her.

"Fudge on your father's budget," her stepmother declared. "This is important. But if we get him back, you must be more careful, Margaret! This match would be more than I ever dreamed for you. You must curb these wild tendencies of yours."

"Wild tendencies?" Margaret scoffed. "If one race is enough to scare off the marquis, he isn't the man I took him for."

"One race, dancing with him so soon after he had broken off with Lady Janice, making eyes at him the very night he was seen courting her. Do you want to appear fast?"

"No one with any sense would call me fast, madame," Margaret assured her. "Unless of course one was referring to my riding."

"You may laugh all you like. Such a name will do you no good."

"No one uses that name. I believe the term being used is *Original*."

Her stepmother paled. "I never thought I'd see the day when someone close to me would wear that appellation. I have obviously failed in my duty."

Much as she often ignored the woman's acerbic council, Margaret could not help but be touched by the note of pathos in her voice. She threw her arms around her stepmother and hugged her fiercely.

"You have not failed. I know you want the best for me. I cannot tell you why I'm different. Perhaps I did not wish to be compared with cousin Genevieve or cousin Allison. Perhaps, like Father, I don't like being a second-rate Munroe. My cousins are in all ways perfect, as you know. I will never be so. Please don't fret, madame. I may not always agree with you as I don't in this instance, but that does not mean I don't recognize that you care for me. I care for you too. But what you ask I simply cannot do. I cannot be less than I am."

As Margaret released her, Mrs. Munroe sighed deeply. "I'm not asking you to be less, Margaret. I am asking you to be more. Why, just once in your life, can you not follow society's dictates? I am not asking you to commit some heinous crime. Just purport yourself as a lady until the marquis is safely engaged to you."

Margaret frowned. "I do not see that I'm fundamentally different from others. What exactly are you asking of me?"

She was immediately sorry she had sounded conciliatory. "You must stop racing," Helen declared. "In fact, it might be best if you do not ride at all. Carriage rides are calmer, and more cozy. Don't you dare take the reins. And you must stop being so effusive when you dance. Sit out a few of the dances and try to move with some moderation when you do join in. You mustn't be seen to perspire. And please refrain from waltzing, even if the hostess is brash enough to allow it. Most of all, keep silent about this latest charity of yours, this Comfort House. What a horrible name! If Lady Jersey had not pledged to support it, I would insist that you quit immediately. I don't care what the Whattlings think of it! You know how embarrassing it is to me. I cannot believe the marquis would countenance it. When you're the Marchioness DeGuis, you can do as you like. I daresay you can build those women a quiet place in the country where no one will have to see them ever again. Until then, you simply cannot afford to say that you know anything about them."

Margaret made a gagging noise and crossed her eyes. Her stepmother gasped at her rudeness. She shook her head in disgust. "Let me see. What you are asking is that I pretend to be someone else entirely; someone quiet, boring, stuffy, priggish; someone just like Lady Janice Willstencraft, who refused him. I'm sure that will endear me to his heart."

"Well," her stepmother sniffed with a blush, "your regular behavior certainly won't endear you to him."

Margaret shook her head again, this time in determination. "That is where you are wrong. He has seen me dance and claimed to like it. He calls my laugh delightful. He admitted enjoying our race today. I am beginning to think that it is the very fact that I *am* different that attracts him to me."

Mrs. Munroe pouted, obviously doubtful. Margaret continued on doggedly. "I may not know as much about society as you do, but I know one thing." She looked down into the woman's stormy brown eyes. "No man appreciates a dishonest bargain. He will hardly come to cherish a wife he married under false pretenses. And do not ask me to forego all my pleasures simply to marry well. I cannot imagine anything more dismal. No, if the Marquis DeGuis decides to marry me, he will do so because he loves me, just as I am, and no other."

She could see the fire of righteousness in her stepmother's eyes and knew she was in for a fight. Even as she squared her shoulders to do battle, there was an embarrassed cough from the doorway. Mrs. Munroe looked past her and Margaret turned to see Becky. The little brown-haired serving girl dropped into a hasty curtsy.

"Beggin' yer pardon, mum, but there's a young lady here to see Miss Margaret and she's wearing a closed bonnet."

Margaret could feel her stepmother scowling at her back. "Who would visit without wanting us to know who she is? If this is about your charity, Margaret, you will put her out at once! I told you I would not have one of them showing up here."

"None of the ladies of Comfort House would care to visit, knowing your censure," Margaret replied with annoyance. "They have been taught their places, far too well. Though why you should be so unfeeling when they are simply trying to put their lives back in order is beyond me. We should commend them, not condemn them. It is only Christian."

"We will speak of this later," Mrs. Munroe hissed. Raising her voice, she continued to Becky. "Did Margaret's caller give you a card, Becky?"

The maid shook her head, but tiptoed into the room and spoke with lowered voice. "No, mum, and she wouldn't give me her name neither."

"You see!" Helen declared accusingly. "Send her away at once."

"No," Margaret ordered, rising. "If Annie Turner, who manages Comfort House, was forced to come here, something terrible must have happened. I'll see her immediately."

Mrs. Munroe surged to her feet as well. "Then you will see her alone. I refuse to lower myself to that level. I'm going to tell your father about this, Margaret. Perhaps he can make you see the danger." She started from the room, then looked back with a warning glance. "And you keep that creature out of my formal withdrawing room!"

Margaret sighed, nodding to the wide-eyed Becky to show the woman in. A moment later, to the whisper of fine silk, her visitor swept into the sitting room. The quality of her sable-trimmed pelisse and matching muff told Margaret immediately that this was not Annie Turner. Even as she was relieved there was no emergency, her curiosity rose. She peered closer and the woman turned her head to prevent her from seeing into the confines of the tightly shaped bonnet.

"Might we speak privately?" she murmured so low that Margaret could not make out the voice. Annie had told her that some of the women who could have retired to Comfort House made impossibly large sums of money for their work. Perhaps she was about to save the soul of a high-priced courtesan. Swallowing, she motioned Becky from the room and sank onto the sofa. The woman closed the sitting room door then turned, lifting a hand to her bonnet. Margaret leaned forward expectantly. As the silk cage of the bonnet was lifted away, two emerald green eyes glared at her, narrowed and cat-like.

"Lady Janice," Margaret acknowledged, not knowing whether to be disappointed or surprised.

The lady stalked farther into the room, tossing the bonnet disdainfully onto a chair. "Do you have any idea what you're doing?" the dark-haired beauty demanded.

"Perching in my sitting room wondering why you are in disguise," Margaret quipped.

"As if I want any more gossip," Lady Janice

sneered. "They would all think I came to beg you to return him to me."

Margaret barked out a laugh that only made the woman's scowl deepen. "As I haven't stolen the Marquis DeGuis," she replied, "I don't see how I can give him back."

"I wouldn't want him if you did," Lady Janice declared vehemently.

Margaret leaned back on the sofa and eyed her. Lady Janice was two years her junior, but she had been a close friend to Allison and Margaret while Allison had been in town. For the last year, however, Janice had moved in more exalted circles, circles that had no use for an Original like Margaret. It had cut a little to learn how cheaply Janice counted their friendship. Now Margaret wasn't sure whether to claim Janice as a friend, especially since her refusal of Thomas had put them at cross-purposes.

At the moment, Janice did not seem to think so either. All of her five-foot, five-inch frame was trembling as if in indignation. She stood with head high and chin raised righteously. She would have been the very picture of a woman scorned if it had not been for the pallor of her face and the red rims of her eyes.

"Me thinks the lady doth protest too much," Margaret said quietly. "Why don't you sit down and tell me why you're here?"

Lady Janice let out a prodigious sigh and slumped onto a chair across from Margaret. "Oh, Margaret, what a crashing disappointment! I thought I'd found my match at last. He seemed so perfect!"

As Margaret still considered him as close to perfection as any man was capable, she did not argue. However, her curiosity rose again. "What happened to change your mind?"

Lady Janice colored. "That is a private matter. But when I heard he had called on you, I knew I had to warn you. We were friends once, and I would not want to see you hurt. Margaret, do not be taken in by him. He will not make you happy."

"That I can well believe," Margaret admitted, thinking of her stepmother's advice to behave in a constricted manner to win the marquis' love. "Much as I admire him, I wonder whether we could possibly suit. We are so different, in temperament, in philosophy."

Lady Janice waved those considerations away with her hand. "I do not doubt you will find him congenial. I am far more demanding than you are, and I was delighted with him."

"So delighted you refused him," Margaret pointed out, annoyed with her cavalier manner. "Are you certain this isn't a case of sour grapes?"

"Not in the slightest," Lady Janice replied, green eyes snapping fire. "I fully intended to marry him, until he showed me he was less than a man."

Margaret started, frown returning. "What do you mean?"

Lady Janice hesitated, then shrugged. "I have a test my suitors must pass. A very personal test. He failed, miserably." She paused again, watching Margaret. As Margaret seldom made any attempt to hide her emotions, she was certain her confusion and curiosity must be showing on her face.

"You understand why he so quickly switched his affections?" Lady Janice asked suddenly.

Margaret chuckled. "Certainly. You refused him. His pride was wounded. I was a sympathetic ear."

"I do not doubt he could find any number of sympathetic ears," Lady Janice replied. "No, Margaret, he is getting desperate."

"Thank you so much for the compliment," Margaret quipped. "I am finding this conversation less and less interesting. You have braved the dangers of gossip to warn me the marquis is less than perfect. It was nobly done. You will pardon me if I disagree."

Lady Janice surged to her feet. "I knew you would be impossible! Any other young lady would have avoided him at all costs so soon after he had been refused."

"Any other young lady would have leapt at the chance to take your place in his affections," Margaret corrected her, rising also. "I assure you, I did not leap. I'm sorry to be mulish, Lady Janice, but it appears to me that you came to warn me off because you want him back. If you love him, tell him so. If you don't, you mustn't mind if others decide to be seen with him."

"I came with the best of intentions," Lady Janice protested, snatching up her bonnet. "As usual, you must play the Original. Learn the lesson to your sorrow." She crammed the bonnet back onto her head with no regard to her artfully arranged coiffure and finished her speech from its depths. "If you will not believe me, ask your cousin Allison. I advised her to use my test. It is my belief that when she did, she preferred to wed a country nobody to the Marquis DeGuis."

"I will write Allison, if I get the opportunity," Margaret allowed. Much as she hated to admit it to Lady Janice, her curiosity had not abated. Something had happened to scare the woman off the scent. It remained to be seen whether that something would also frighten Margaret. "You are certain you cannot simply explain this test?"

Lady Janice finished settling the bonnet. "It is personal. And, forgive my bluntness, but you have a reputation of being unable to tell a lie. I should not like it bandied about that I am less than a lady. Which I am not," she hastily added.

"Very well." Margaret sighed. "But you must understand that without evidence to the contrary, I must stand fast on my opinion of the marquis."

Lady Janice reached for the door. "You'll have your evidence. You are too passionate to do otherwise. And when you know the truth, you will never agree to wed the marquis. I only hope you find out before it's too late!"

Seven

Margaret was still on his mind when Thomas took dinner that evening with his sister and aunt. He found himself eyeing his diminutive sister halfway up the long, polished mahogany dining table. In her unruffled gown of lavender silk she did not seem the type to frighten her soon-to-be-fiancé Lord Darton as Margaret occasionally frightened Thomas. Of course, Lady Catherine DeGuis lacked most of the attributes that made Margaret Munroe impressive. His sister was barely five feet tall, her hair was a long straight sunny blond, and her figure was willowy. While her eyes were blue, it was a deep, warm color that always made her appear wide-eyed. Her nose was a little snubby thing and her laugh was a rare and polite little giggle. He could not imagine his fellow peer ever being discomposed in her presence.

His Aunt Agnes at the far end of the table, however, was another story. While she was as small as his sister, and even more fragile at the age of seventy-two, her iron-gray hair and gray-blue eyes marked a strength of purpose that was as strong as steel. As a child, he had been intimidated by her sharp voice and piercing gaze. He could never seem to behave properly in her presence; something was always lacking. He was almost immune to her scolds now, although Catherine had yet to learn to tell the woman her commanding advice was not needed.

Tonight was no exception. He had no sooner picked up his damask napkin than his aunt started in at him.

"Have you broken off with that Willstencraft chit?" she demanded before the footmen could start serving the food. "I thought you intended to propose a week ago. What happened?"

Catherine paled, refusing to lift her eyes from the figured bone china in front of her, clearly embarrassed by their aunt's probing.

Thomas took a deep breath. "Lady Janice decided we didn't suit," he replied, signaling to the nearest fellow to serve him from the plate of beef ragout. "I am no longer welcome to call."

"Oh, Thomas," Catherine murmured kindly as the footman lay some of the beef on her plate as well. "I'm so sorry."

"Thank you, Catherine," he replied, smiling at her bowed head. "I assure you, I'll be fine."

"So fine you immediately start in anew," his aunt interjected with a huff. "What's this I hear about you taking up with the Munroes again? I thought you'd learned your lesson with the younger sister. Must you be abused by the cousin as well?"

He kept a polite smile on his face and waved away the salmon. "Miss Munroe is a welcome change from my previous interactions with the fair sex."

Catherine caught her breath. "Then you are truly courting her?"

"Don't be ridiculous," Aunt Agnes snapped. "He couldn't be serious."

Thomas found his temper flaring. He set down his fork and scowled at his aunt at the far end of the table. "And if I am? What would be wrong with court-ing Margaret Munroe?"

He was immediately sorry he had asked, for his aunt was obviously delighted to inform him. "She's an Original! I need not remind you that the term is reserved for those whose foibles are so outstanding as to be a constant source of entertainment to the ton. Is that what you want in a marchioness?"

"I can think of worse things than to be constantly entertained," he countered. Remembering how much he had enjoyed their race that morning, and the way she had made him enjoy himself even after Lady Janice's refusal, he knew the statement to be more than a loyal defense.

"I doubt you would be entertained for long," his aunt replied. "Already I've heard the most shocking story about her."

A part of him quailed. After his last attempt at courting, he had begun to hope this time might be different. Certainly the woman was different from anyone he had ever met. Was he now to find that she was totally unsuitable as well?

"What have you heard?" he demanded.

Lady Agnes cast her niece a look of triumph, and Catherine bit her lower lip. Apparently his sister knew the tale as well and didn't think he should be told. His feeling of foreboding increased.

"We were told," his aunt informed him, "that she was seen racing this very morning in Hyde Park, with a man!"

"Lady Whitworth implied she was racing you," Catherine put in quietly. "But of course we assured her you would never be so vulgar as to race a woman, nor so foolhardy as to race in the park."

Thomas tried to summon the guilt that should ac-company the fact that the ton was gossiping about his foolhardy and vulgar behavior. But, to his surprise, he could not seem to awaken his conscience. The memory still hung bright and joy-filled. The only twinge came from the fact that he had nearly missed the joy because of an attitude very like theirs.

"You need not have demurred," he told them. "I did race Miss Munroe in the park this morning. As there were few people about, it seemed neither vulgar nor unsafe. I had a marvelous time."

Lady Agnes stared at him, and Catherine's already wide eyes were impossibly huge.

"Then, then you intend to continue this connection?" his aunt sputtered.

"Most assuredly," Thomas replied, spearing a mouthful of the beef. Lady Agnes continued to sputter for a few moments, then launched into an impassioned diatribe about the proper way to conduct a courtship. As she had never married, he found her advice without basis. He let her continue to rail throughout the meal, knowing she would only be happy if she thought she was making her point clear. He was equally happy letting the noise wash over him. Only when he excused himself for his club did Catherine speak again.

"I think it very noble of you, Thomas, to stand up for your true love," she proclaimed.

Lady Agnes snorted. "True love? True insanity if you ask me. Like should marry like, my boy. You have always prided yourself on a well-reasoned response to matters. You may find this wildness attractive now, but it will pale in the long run."

"Only time will tell, Aunt," he replied, dropping a kiss on his sister's head for her support. Even as he did so, he felt a twinge of guilt. He could not in good conscience say that he was pursuing an interest in Margaret Munroe out of a sudden passionate love.

His aunt was probably right when she said it was the novelty of it that attracted him. Yet he saw no reason why that couldn't lead to a good marriage, in the end.

Catherine looked up at him in surprise, coloring at his gesture. He smiled encouragement and headed for the quiet of White's.

But he was not to be given any peace even in his favorite club. No sooner had he begun his stroll through the card room when he sighted Reginald Pinstin bearing down on him, wide mouth grinning as if they were old friends.

Thomas would not give in to the panic to flee. He squared his shoulders and raised his quizzing glass. Pinstin skidded to a stop, grin fading.

"Are you peeved with me, my lord?" he whined, paling. His full lower lip trembled as pathetically as a young girl's on being denied a new bauble. "Truly I thought you would enjoy courting my cousin, Margaret."

The card players at the nearest table paused in their play to listen to the drama. Thomas turned his glare on them, and the pasteboard squares flew back into action. He jerked his head for Pinstin to follow him and led the fellow to two chairs in a quiet corner.

"I would prefer, Mr. Pinstin," he said, pausing to frown quellingly, "that you refrain from linking your cousin's name with mine."

Reggie had clearly been expecting some other confidence, for his color, which had been returning, fled once more. "I feared this. She is her own worst enemy. Have pity on her, my lord and forgive whatever sin she has committed. She'll make you a fine wife, truly."

Thomas did not want the fellow bandying it about that he was disappointed in Margaret, especially since the opposite was quite true. On the other hand, he didn't much like confirming anyone's suspicions that his intentions were serious. He wasn't sure that they were. Curse Pinstin for being so adept at putting him in untenable positions.

"What I feel for your cousin, Mr. Pinstin," he tried with his most determined voice, "is none of your affair. It was good of you to introduce us, but I reserve the right to proceed from here keeping my own council. Now, excuse me, for I have friends I should meet."

"Oh?" Pinstin licked his lips eagerly, gaze darting about. "Perhaps I could join you? I have a number of stories I could relate regarding my cousin."

Thomas refused to say another word on the subject to an encroaching toady like Reginald Pinstin, cousin or no. He was about to tell the fellow so when he spotted Court entering the room. He managed to catch his friend's eye easily enough, but when the viscount saw Thomas' companion, he hurried in the opposite direction. *Coward,* Thomas thought.

"No, I must go," Thomas told Pinstin, rising. Pinstin puckered up again, then brightened.

"Then perhaps a toast," he caroled, springing to his feet as well and signaling a passing waiter. "To my cousin Margaret."

Thomas was determined not to be drawn into the fellow's snare again. "As your cousin is beyond peer," he quipped, "a mere toast would be an insult. Good night, Mr. Pinstin."

Pinstin was doing his fish imitation again, but Thomas turned his back on him and strode after Court.

He eventually found the viscount in the farthest room from the door, lounging in a wing-back chair, eyeing the fire, brandy at his elbow.

"Driven you to drink, has he?" Thomas asked with a chuckle as he sank into the seat opposite his friend.

Court managed a smile, straightening. "Sorry, DeGuis. I can't abide the fellow. Two rescues in less than a fortnight seemed excessive."

"Agreed," Thomas replied. "You don't mind if I join you? I could use some peace and quiet."

"Certainly." Court's smile faded. "Though you must allow me to apologize. I heard Pinstin created a scene at the Baminger's ball after I left with your sister. I understand you actually had to call on Miss Munroe because of it. You must believe I would never have abandoned you if I had known."

"On the contrary," Thomas replied readily. "I told the fellow I appreciated the introduction, even if his method left something to be desired. I appear to have been too narrow in my choice of ladies to pursue. Miss Munroe is a welcome change."

Court eyed him, iron eyes reflecting the fire. "Welcome? Do you mean that?"

Thomas raised an eyebrow at the implied challenge. In truth, he was beginning to tire of the fact that everyone assumed Margaret Munroe was somehow beneath him. He found her diverting at the least and disarmingly charming at the best. "Am I known for lying to my friends?" he quipped.

"Never," Court replied. He returned his gaze to the fire. "I am simply surprised it has gone this far. Will you court her?"

"I am considering it," Thomas answered stiffly. Hearing the belligerence in his tone, he forced himself to relax. "That is, I am uncertain. She is different from anyone I have ever met."

"Different does not mean better," Court murmured.

"Don't tell me you're against her as well?" Thomas frowned.

To his surprise, Court colored. "The lady is not my type. She beat me in a private horse race last year, a claiming race no less. She's the one who won my prize three-year-old. Her father made her give it back, but I can tell you it was embarrassing nonetheless. Good thing it was off-season."

"Her parents allowed her to race you?" Thomas asked, even more surprised.

Court tightened his jaw. "I don't believe her stepmother knew. Her father sent back a note with the horse. It wasn't an apology."

Thomas shook his head. "I had no idea. She challenged me to a friendly race today, but it was not for a prize. I couldn't resist the offer. I'm surprised you accepted."

"Prestwick issued the invitation on behalf of a 'friend.' I assumed it was for Lord Leslie Petersborough. The two are nearly inseparable, and you know Petersborough's father the marquis frowns on his son racing. Besides, she was dressed as a coachman and that black beast of hers wouldn't let me get close enough to see her face beneath the cap. It wasn't until it was over and she'd won that I knew."

There was the unmistakable trace of bitterness in his friend's voice. Thomas wondered if he'd feel so angry if Margaret had beaten him. It did not seem likely, but then he could not imagine mistaking her bustline for that of a man, coachman's cape or no. He decided against mentioning it to Court.

"Well," he said with a shrug, "no harm done. As I said, the lady is a refreshing change."

"Then you're done with Lady Janice?" Court asked.

"Quite done," Thomas assured him.

"Pity," Court murmured. "I thought surely you had her, old fellow. You seemed well matched. But perhaps it is all to the good. She is developing quite a reputation for turning fellows down. You're number twelve, did you know that?"

Hearing that he had eleven comrades somehow did not make him feel any better. He was certain they could not have been discharged for the same ignoble reason, certainly not by two different women. "I wish the lady well," he replied. "I can only hope her next suitor is more successful."

"If any man can be successful," Court muttered darkly. "I begin to think Pinstin has the right of it. Women are a fickle lot."

"What do you mean?" Thomas demanded, eyes narrowing as he realized the man must be talking about his sister. "Has something happened between you and Catherine?"

"No," Court hedged, refusing to meet his eye. "I mean, nothing is happening. That is precisely the problem. Your sister seems to have taken a dislike to me."

"Why would that be?" Thomas asked quietly. Court would have had to have been an idiot not to hear the threat under the words. He was not an idiot.

He sat straighter. "I did nothing improper, I assure you. I know the difference between an opera dancer and a lady like your sister. We've gone driving twice and she brought her maid along each time. Whenever I've called, your aunt has played chaperone. Whenever you've allowed me to take her out, once to the opera and the other night to the ball, you've been in attendance for much of the time."

"Are you saying you haven't had sufficient time alone with her?" Thomas probed with a frown.

"It doesn't matter," Court replied. "The few moments we have had alone are the same as when we are in company. She refuses to say more than three words at a time to me, and they are generally, 'yes, my lord,' and 'no, my lord.' It's incredibly difficult to get to know a young lady well enough to propose in such an atmosphere."

"You must try harder to draw her out," Thomas advised, relieved to hear that there appeared to have been nothing to hurt his sister. "I told you, she is very sensitive."

"I've been as gentle as a lamb, I assure you," Court insisted. He eyed Thomas for a moment. "You're certain there isn't someone else?"

Thomas started. In truth, he had paid little attention to his sister's activities or visitors, assuming the matter taken care of by his agreement with Court. If Catherine had fallen in love with another suitor, it would explain her antipathy for the young viscount and her sudden championship of his courtship of a woman she assumed to be his true love.

"I'll speak to my sister," he promised. "My own courting has taken precedence, and for that I apologize."

"You must do what you can to set up your line," Court agreed. "A collapse like the one you had last winter would make any man feel mortal."

Thomas frowned at him.

Court kept the gaze. "Do not bridle. I assure you I have told no one of the incident. I wouldn't even have known you were sick from the way you put down dinner that night. There is nothing like your Mrs. Tate's famous fish chowder. And that physician you had in to interview you afterward said it was a freak occurrence."

"As long as I do nothing that would unduly excite my heart, whatever that means," Thomas agreed glumly.

"Precisely. You do not live a particularly sedate life, old fellow, though I would hardly call you reckless. I only mention the incident to show you that I understand what's driving you to find a marchioness and set up your nursery. As I said, any man would feel so driven under the circumstances. But are you sure about Margaret Munroe, old fellow?"

Thomas sighed. "I wish I knew. In truth, I'm tiring of all this. I'd like the matter settled. Margaret Munroe seems no worse than any other and considerably better than some."

Court nodded. "Then perhaps we can dispense with the ladies and discuss something of more importance. You have been preoccupied of late, but our friends in Parliament do not understand your silence on the proposed amendment to the Poor Laws. Lord Liverpool was especially concerned."

Thomas felt a twinge of guilt. He had never had much patience with the lords who played at governing—appearing and disappearing from the House as the mood took them. It appalled him that of the hundreds of seats in the hall, fewer than a third were ever occupied in a given session. Perhaps that was why it took no more than three nobles to make a quorum. But allowing decisions about governance of the commonwealth to rest in so few hands was surely a dangerous thing. He should have been more attentive.

"Please convey my apologies to the Prime Minister," Thomas told the viscount. "I did not realize the bill was coming to a vote."

"Oh, it isn't," Court replied, and again Thomas heard the trace of bitterness. "That is precisely the problem. This business of celebrating the end of the war has turned everyone's heads. The cabinet has yet to formally introduce the bill to discussion. They want support to be assured before then. Have you seen the proposed language?"

When Thomas shook his head, the viscount continued. "I'll have my secretary drop by a copy. It's a sweeping gesture, designed to rid our streets of the trash we seem to be accumulating."

"It's difficult for me to equate humanity with trash," Thomas remarked.

Court eyed him, iron gaze unreadable. "It wouldn't if you noticed the wastrels begging on the street corners. It's an embarrassment to a civilized nation like ours."

"On that we agree," Thomas replied with equal determination. "But it is the method of removing them from the streets that is the problem. I will not countenance workhouses."

The fire was dancing in the viscount's eyes. "Nor will I countenance useless charity. A man should work for his wages."

"And should the women and children?" Thomas pressed.

Court stiffened. "I can see we have different views on the matter."

Thomas was used to seeing the man bridle about political issues. Court had his eye on the prime minister position someday, if he could prove himself more able than Lord Malcolm Breckonridge, the leader of the moderate Whigs, who were growing in popularity. But much as he wanted to support his friend, he would not change his principles.

"Our differences are nothing two civilized gentlemen cannot discuss, I hope," Thomas tried in mollification.

Court retrieved his glass of brandy and raised it in salute. "Not at all. I look forward to changing your mind."

"As do I," Thomas replied. "About the Poor Laws, and Margaret Munroe."

Eight

Margaret did not immediately pen a note to her cousin Allison. Between her conversation with her stepmother and the one with Lady Janice, she had much to think about. She was not given the opportunity, however, for no sooner had she seen Lady Janice to the front door than Mrs. Munroe was at her side.

"Well?" she demanded. "Who was she? Why did she seek you out here?"

"She was not one of the women from Comfort House," Margaret assured her. "And I see no reason to keep her identity a secret, even if she guards it so closely. You will not gossip, will you, madame?"

Her stepmother drew herself up to her full height, just under Margaret's chin. "Certainly not!" Then she bent closer conspiratorially, dark eyes alight, voice lowered. "Who was it?"

"Lady Janice Willstencraft," Margaret replied, turning to lead her wide-eyed stepmother back to the sitting room.

"Lady Janice?" Mrs. Munroe frowned in obvious confusion as she lowered herself onto the sofa. Before Margaret could explain, she brightened again. "Lady Janice! Why, my dear, you have obviously won. Why would she come in disguise but to beg you to

return the marquis?" Just as quickly as she had
brightened, she sobered again. "I certainly hope you
did not agree, Margaret. I know your tendency to be
kind-hearted. Promise me you did not return him to
her."

"I am considerably tired of everyone making as-
sumptions," Margaret declared. "The Marquis De-
Guis is not a book, madame. He does not belong to
Lady Janice, nor does he belong to me."

"I can only hope you did not tell *her* that," her
stepmother answered with a sniff.

"I did not have to," Margaret explained. "She did
not wish to renew the acquaintance. She advised me
to shun him as well."

Mrs. Munroe's frown deepened. "Did she say
why?"

"She hinted at some dire flaw in his character, but
refused to name it."

Now her stepmother paled. "Could he be a mon-
ster under that civility? Do you think he struck her
or attempted to force her?"

Margaret shrugged, though her heart quailed at
the thought that her hero could be so depraved. "In
truth, I don't know what to think. As vain as it sounds,
I would be tempted to put it down to a case of jeal-
ousy, except she advised me to contact cousin Allison
for particulars."

"Is that why Allison turned him down?" her stepmother asked, clearly amazed. "It would certainly explain her preference for the Pentercast boy, though
a second son of a country squire is still sinking rather
low. I will pen your aunt immediately."

"No," Margaret said. "Aunt Ermintrude is nothing
if not close-mouthed. I doubt she would tell you. Besides, I'm not sure she knows either. It sounds as if

it were some kind of pact between Lady Janice and Allison. I'll write Allison."

Mrs. Munroe nodded, rising. "It is settled, then. I expect you to let me know the minute you get an answer. And until you do, I intend to see you are more closely chaperoned."

Margaret frowned. "Do you think that necessary? He has never been less than a gentleman with me."

"I do not wish to find he is anything less. But I also do not want anything to happen to you, Margaret. I have never heard anything bad about DeGuis, mind you, unless of course one counts that business about their hearts. Still, I refuse to take chances."

The word "heart" hung in Margaret's mind. "What about their hearts?" she pressed, thinking again of her fear that her hero might not be able to love deeply.

Her stepmother waved a hand. "The last marquis, and his father if memory serves, died rather early from weak hearts, or so the story goes. I'm sure it's why the present marquis is so set on finding a bride and assuring his line. He cannot be certain how much time he has."

"But he seems so strong," Margaret protested, re-alizing this was the source of the desperation Lady Janice had tried to warn her about. "He rides daily. He races!"

"Certainly he appears healthier than his father," Helen acknowledged. "And with a conscientious wife to watch over him, he will surely live longer than his predecessors. You need not worry that you will be a widow soon, dear."

Margaret raised an eyebrow. "I am not even en-gaged and you have me wearing the black. I think I will simply forget this conversation, if you please."

But she found as her stepmother left and she sat

at the writing table that she could not forget. Lady Janice Willstencraft had been as intent on her search for a perfect husband as the marquis had been intent on his search for a bride. She had to have found something horrible in Thomas to have refused him. Yet she and Margaret were so different. Was it possible that what repelled Lady Janice would not bother Margaret in the slightest? She could hardly wait to see what her cousin had to say.

Her note to Allison was brief and to the point. Even in writing she saw no need to dissemble.

"Dear cousin Allison," she wrote. "You may have heard that the Marquis DeGuis, your old fiancé, has shown interest in me. I am nearly as surprised as you must be. You may also have heard that before this, he was courting Lady Janice Willstencraft. She visited me today to explain why she had refused him. He apparently failed some test. She assures me that he failed a similar test with you. She refused to explain this test to me, and advised I ask you for particulars. Can you please tell me anything you know about the marquis that might make me think twice about being courted by him, much less marrying him? Part of me doubts it will ever reach that point, but it never hurts to be prepared.

"I hope all is well with you. Please give my good wishes to cousin Genevieve and Aunt Ermintrude, as well as your husband. I await your word. Margaret."

As she sealed the note and rang for Becky, she wondered whether she should have told Allison how important the answer was to her. Yet, somehow, she still could not bear to confess to her cousin that she was in love with the marquis. She could only hope that Allison would know that anything having to do with courtship was a serious matter.

She was relieved that her stepmother did not push

the subject any more that day. She was even more pleased that no one saw fit to mention it at dinner that night or breakfast the following morning. Her stepmother was obviously deep in thought trying to determine what dire secret the marquis kept, and her father was quite oblivious to the entire affair. It was nice having one relative who did not badger her.

She returned from a constitutional around the square shortly after lunch to find a crested carriage waiting at her door. That the leaping lion belonged to the Marquis DeGuis only made her hurry up the steps, heart jumping just as high as the beast. She was therefore disappointed to find not the marquis when she peered into the elegant withdrawing room but two women she did not recognize. The older of the two was just as capable as Thomas of sitting stiffly in the chairs as if they were thrones. The younger slumped a bit as if wishing she were elsewhere. Still, just the fact that they were in the withdrawing room was indication of their status. Knowing her stepmother would have apoplexy if she attempted to sit on the best upholstery in her street wear, she hurried to her room to change. By the time she returned a few minutes later, Helen was as pale as blancmange.

"So, this must be your daughter," the older woman said with a frown as Margaret entered and went to sit next to her stepmother on the sofa. Mrs. Munroe's eyes were glassy, but she blinked and gazed at Margaret in such a pleading manner that Margaret knew she was being asked once again to behave as society dictated. Accordingly, she pasted on a polite smile and responded, "Yes, I'm Margaret Munroe. I don't believe I've had the pleasure."

"Lady Agnes DeGuis," her stepmother managed in a choked voice, "and Lady Catherine DeGuis, may I present my daughter, Miss Margaret Munroe?"

Margaret nodded with deference to the older woman and the pale young woman who sat opposite her. The young woman looked almost as uncomfortable as her stepmother, fidgeting in the stiff chair as if it confined the skirts of her sky-blue silk morning dress. Lady Agnes shook out the skirts of her brown striped silk walking dress as if she wished to disavow having met Margaret.

"So, you are the creature who has captured my nephew's attentions."

Mrs. Munroe sucked in a breath, eyes tortured.

Margaret met the woman's gaze unfalteringly, once again wavering between annoyance and amusement. "The only creatures associated with this house are in the mews at the end of the lane. And your nephew has much better taste in horses."

Lady Agnes' eyes narrowed. "I thought he also had better taste in women."

"Ah, yes, the two diamonds of the first water, who refused him," Margaret acknowledged, giving way to annoyance. "But where are my manners? Might I get you anything? Tea? Lemonade? Hemlock?"

"Margaret," her stepmother gave a strangled cry, hand fluttering to her chest.

Lady Agnes quirked a smile. "Your point, Miss Munroe. If I expect courtesy, I must give it. You are not what I expected."

"And what did you expect?" Margaret asked, curious of the tales told of her.

"Someone with considerably less wit. The term 'Original' often masks a feeble mind that has found a way to be entertaining. I do not sense that in you." She leaned forward, gaze intensifying not unlike her nephew's. "You realize how dangerous it would be for my nephew to marry an Original? The DeGuis are known for their good breeding, their reserve, their endless propriety. They are examples to whom all others aspire. Can you manage that, I wonder?"

"Heavens, why would I want to try?" Margaret replied truthfully. "An Original they may call me, but I'd prefer originality to conformity. If I'm not good enough to be a DeGuis, perhaps I should remain a Munroe."

Lady Agnes sat back, stiff-lipped. Mrs. Munroe moaned audibly. Lady Catherine looked stricken.

"Then you don't return my brother's love?" she cried.

Margaret started, eyes widening. "Your brother's love? Does he claim to love me?" Despite all her stern talks with herself, her heart leapt at the very thought.

"He does not," Lady Agnes snapped, glaring her niece to silence. She returned her gaze to Margaret. "Thomas is, in all things, the keeper of his own council. The question is, are you in love with my nephew?"

Margaret felt every eye in the room on her. Her own code of conduct said she must answer truthfully. Her sense of self-preservation warned her to lie through her teeth.

"Certainly I would only marry if I were in love," she hedged.

"And would you marry my nephew if he asked?" Lady Agnes pressed, blue-gray eyes bright. "I will not have him abused again."

"I would have to be assured of his love as well," Margaret replied, spine stiff. The perspiration her stepmother had warned her not to have was running down her back.

Lady Agnes was leaning forward again, nostrils flared like a hound to the scent. "No more round-aboutation, young lady. My nephew has been through entirely enough of this nonsense in the last year. Are you willing to be his marchioness?"

Mrs. Munroe held her breath. Lady Catherine pressed her lips tightly together as if to keep from crying out. Lady Agnes glared in challenge.

Margaret spread her hands. "If Lord DeGuis can keep his own council, so can I. He hasn't asked me. Until he does, I have nothing more to say in the matter."

Lady Agnes rose in a flurry of skirts. "Then this visit is at an end. Come, Catherine."

Lady Catherine rose just as hurriedly, but as she trailed out the door after her aunt, she glanced back at Margaret with a frown, as if questioning her resolve. Or perhaps her sanity. Mrs. Munroe leapt up and hurried after them, wringing her hands and babbling incoherently. Margaret did not rise from the sofa.

When her stepmother returned a few minutes later, Margaret stiffened her back and her intentions.

"Oh, Margaret," was all Helen managed to say, sinking onto the sofa beside her.

Margaret patted her hands. In truth, she wasn't sure what to think. She ought to feel depressed or abused, but all she could seem to feel was exhilarated. She had met the worst the enemy could provide and she had survived. "Don't worry, madame. I said I wanted the marquis to marry me as I am. Now he'll simply have a very good report of exactly the kind of woman he's getting."

Nine

Thomas received the report that night over dinner. "You went and visited Miss Munroe?" He frowned at his aunt's announcement of the fact even as the footmen served out the dinner. "I was not aware you were acquainted."

"We are not." Lady Agnes sniffed, settling herself back against the Chippendale chair so firmly that her navy silk dress rustled. "And for good reason. I do not comport myself with Originals."

Thomas refrained from mentioning that his aunt had enough foibles to be considered an Original herself. "I certainly hope you did not call her that."

"She did," Catherine put in with a sigh.

Thomas raised an eyebrow. "I see. Perhaps you had better tell me the whole of it. It sounds as if I will have to apologize for my family."

Lady Agnes' eyes glittered. "Do not apologize for me. I did what I thought was in your best interest. I will not countenance the destruction of the DeGuis name. Nor will I stand by while you emulate yourself on the wiles of these conniving debutantes."

"Miss Munroe is not conniving," Thomas argued, feeling his temper rising yet again. "She is by far the most honest female I have ever met." Determined not to be drawn into another debate on the lady's character, he stabbed a piece of venison and shoved it rather inelegantly into his mouth.

"On that we agree," Lady Agnes replied. "She hasn't the tact to be conniving. She offered me hemlock."

Thomas choked on the venison. "She what?" he managed.

"Aunt was very rude, Thomas," Catherine put in hurriedly, glancing quickly between them. "Miss Munroe was fully justified in answering her in kind."

"Yes, she was," Lady Agnes agreed. "She is intelligent, witty, and not afraid to stand her ground. I think you may have finally found a woman worthy of bearing the DeGuis name, Thomas. You have my permission to marry her."

Catherine stared at her open-mouthed, her own piece of venison falling into the damask napkin on the lap of her mauve silk gown. Thomas felt the fork drop with a clatter from fingers that seemed to have gone as numb as his brain. He shook his head. "Did I hear you correctly? Are you telling me that you actually *liked* Miss Munroe?"

"Intensely," Lady Agnes replied, attacking her meal with gusto. "I greatly look forward to having her in the household. I haven't had someone to spar with since your dear father passed away. Now eat your dinner, Thomas, before it gets cold."

He managed to pick up the fork and return to his eating, though in truth he was no longer sure what else they were having or whether it was well-cooked or not. After defending his interest in Margaret Munroe to all and sundry, he couldn't quite believe that his aunt of all people had suddenly capitulated. He glanced at his sister, who was now poking with equal disinterest at her dinner.

"And how did you like Miss Munroe, Catherine?" he couldn't help asking.

Catherine blushed. "She was quite outspoken, but I am used to that."

"Ha," Lady Agnes barked out in a laugh. "As well you may be living with me all these years."

Thomas was unsatisfied by the answer. He watched his sister closely. "But did you like her?" he pressed.

She met his gaze with a pensive look. "I think there will be times when she frightens me, but I also think there will be times when I greatly admire her spirit. So, yes, I suppose you could say that I like her."

"There," Lady Agnes proclaimed, "we are agreed. Though what poor Catherine will do when she has two of us to contend with, I'm sure I don't know."

Catherine smiled sweetly. "I shall count myself lucky not to have to exert myself in conversation. You and Thomas' lady will carry it all for me."

Thomas eyed her thoughtfully. It was the most his sister had spoken at dinner for a long time. He was ashamed to admit he had not thought to draw her out before. "I'm glad you found her enjoyable, Catherine. But I doubt you will have to worry about making conversation with Aunt Agnes and Miss Munroe. You will be living in your own home soon enough. I understand there is a particular gentleman interested in asking for your hand."

Catherine immediately paled, doing nothing to make Thomas feel any better about the impending match with Court. "I . . . I cannot think who you mean," she stammered, dropping her gaze.

"He means Lord Darton," Lady Agnes put in pointedly.

"Oh." Catherine laughed nervously. "Yes, of course. Lord Darton."

"Is he so easy to forget?" Thomas asked. "I understood he had been rather marked in his attentions."

Lady Agnes snorted. "He has been spotty at best. At least when you court a woman, Thomas, you do not leave anyone in doubt as to your intentions."

"Hasn't Lord Darton made his intentions plain?" Thomas probed with a frown.

"I suppose so," Catherine replied, although she sounded distinctly unsatisfied about the matter. "I believe you are correct that he seems to want to further our acquaintance."

"And how do you feel about that?" Thomas asked.

Catherine shrugged. "He is handsome in his own way. And he seems intelligent. I would not go any farther than that at this time."

"Well, I do not like him, Thomas," Lady Agnes put in with a sniff. "He strikes me as a libertine."

Thomas laid down his fork carefully. "Has he been less than a gentleman to Catherine? I promise you, that will stop immediately."

"No, no," Catherine protested, becoming more agitated. "He is always a gentleman. I simply am not comfortable in his company."

"Another with arrogant opinions," Lady Agnes said with a nod. "She has enough of that in me."

Catherine managed a smile for her aunt. "You know I adore you, Aunt Agnes. But you are right that when I marry, I would prefer a gentler sort of fellow."

Thomas sat back and sighed. Court's passions, running deep and rarely showing, had seemed a perfect match to his sister's. Why couldn't she see that? "It seems to me that Lord Darton is as reserved as they come. If we find a more quiet fellow, the two of you may grow old in silence!"

"But if it is companionable silence, who would mind?" Catherine protested gently.

"Do you truly find so little admirable in him?" Thomas pressed, trying in vain to think of what manly characteristic the fellow lacked. "Most young ladies seem to want to capture his attentions."

"Then I hope they do so," Catherine murmured. "As for me, I am content as things stand."

Lady Agnes was eyeing Thomas with a frown. "Why are you so determined to plead this fellow's case? You haven't made any arrangements with this Darton, have you? I shouldn't like to council Catherine to keep looking if you've made a decision."

Catherine turned an alarmed face to his. Thomas swallowed, but straightened. "You both know it is my intention of arranging Catherine's marriage. She could do a lot worse than Court."

"And I could do a great deal better!" Catherine protested.

Her sudden spirit surprised Thomas. Remembering Darton's conjecture that she had found someone else she preferred, he narrowed his eyes. "And are you prepared to name the candidate?" he challenged.

Catherine exchanged glances with their aunt, took a deep breath, and sat straighter. Thomas waited patiently for her to tell him the name of some obscure scholarly fellow she had set her cap for. "I am not," she said firmly. "But I will not marry Lord Darton. That is my final word on the subject."

Thomas shook his head. "It may be your final word, but it is far from mine. You know Mother and Father were married through an arrangement by their parents, and it was their wish that I make similar arrangements for you. I would like your opinion on the matter, of course, but the final decision will be mine as the head of this family."

Catherine stared at him. He thought for a moment

he had reduced her to tears, and guilt tore at him, but she tossed down her napkin and bolted out of the chair to run from the room. Thomas started up to follow her.

"Sit down," Lady Agnes ordered. He froze, giving her the courtesy of finishing her thought before disobeying her. She sighed. "Please, sit down? I know you're just as worried as I am that the girl has so little spunk. If she has finally chosen to show it, you should be glad."

Thomas sank into his seat. "But I've upset her. I had no idea she so disliked Lord Darton. I suppose it isn't too late to tell him I've changed my mind. Or rather, that Catherine has."

Lady Agnes shook her head. "I'd say nothing at this point. I'm not sure the girl knows her mind. Let her get used to seeing him in this new light. If she still finds him objectionable, then you can send him packing."

"Very well," Thomas agreed with a wry smile. "But I hope you are right."

"I was right about your Miss Munroe, wasn't I?" his aunt all but chortled. "And it does not surprise me that Catherine finds the fellow uncomfortable. He is too cold. As she said, she prefers the kind of gentleman who speaks with his eyes." She shuddered. "Melodramatic nonsense, just as I told that fellow we had in last winter to paint my portrait. Now there was a deep one. Even Catherine remarked on it."

"Whom do you mean?" Thomas asked with a frown.

"Oh, that was when you were up at Hillwater with Lord Darton," his aunt replied. "We were bored beyond anything. Some days I cannot get Catherine to say two words to me, at least not two intelligent words. Lady Whitworth had had this French fellow, Christien

LaTour, I think his name was, paint her portrait, a miniature, actually. It amused Catherine to have one done of me. She's inordinately pleased with it. Keeps it on her bedside table."

"Could she have formed an attachment to this fellow?" Thomas asked, frown deepening.

Lady Agnes shook her head. "That hardly seems likely. A DeGuis and an itinerant artist? Catherine would never be so rash. No, she simply has to get used to seeing Lord Darton in this new light. Leave it to me, my boy. It will all come out right in the end. Perhaps when you're both settled, I can feel myself free to travel at last."

Thomas reluctantly agreed, but over the next two days, he began to regret his decision. He had hoped to call on Margaret the first day, but when Court showed up at the house, Thomas felt he had to stay and visit with him. When Catherine refused to see Court, Thomas felt compelled to talk to his sister, who then refused to see him. It took all his tact and diplomacy to get his sister to agree to see the fellow if he should call again. It took all his tact, diplomacy, and a bottle of champagne to get Court to agree to try again, but only if Thomas consented to go with him. Accordingly, the second day, Thomas played chaperone during the visit and spent the evening encouraging first his sister and then the viscount to continue the courting. He made little headway with either. The best he could get was an agreement from Court to join his family when they repaired to Hillwater, his estate in the Lake District, for August and September.

"Though I don't promise anything will come of it," Court warned. "You know I like the fishing. We can only hope your sister will take a similar liking to me."

By the time he had settled his sister and the viscount, it was the afternoon of the third day. He knew he had to visit Margaret. Surely she must be wondering what had kept him. He had considered writing her, but was concerned that the gesture would be seen as overly familiar by her parents. Which only reminded him that if he was making compromising statements of his intentions to his own relatives, it was more than time he made appropriate statements to hers.

It was looking more and more as if he were meant to court Margaret Munroe. The thought both pleased and concerned him. It had been less than a fortnight since Lady Janice's refusal, after all. He still wasn't ready to lay bare his heart. But perhaps moving from a friendship to courting was not such a big step. He could court the lady as long as he liked, with only rumors should he decide to break it off. He did not need to make an emotional investment yet.

With the idea in mind of speaking to both Mr. Munroe and Margaret that day, he set off for their quiet little house on the edge of Mayfair. Unfortunately, he was doomed to failure there as well. Mr. Munroe was at his club, according to the little maid who answered the door, and Miss Munroe had gone into the city. He handed her his card and started to leave when, with a rustle of skirts, Mrs. Munroe intercepted him.

"Oh, my lord, how good to see you," she caroled. She reached out a hand as if to detain him, then quickly snatched it back as if realizing the gesture was too familiar. "We had thought perhaps, that is, we had wondered, that is, how good to see you."

Thomas bowed to her. "Very good to see you as well, Mrs. Munroe. I hope everyone in your family is well."

"Oh, quite well," she assured him. "Quite well. Yet, perhaps well is too strong a word. I think perhaps you might say we have been saddened not to have your company with us for so many days. It is so very good to see you again."

Thomas bit back a smile. "Very kind of you, I'm sure. I understand Miss Munroe has gone calling."

The woman paled, and Thomas felt his gut clench. He waited to be told that Margaret was out riding or driving or visiting with some other fellow, some more attentive, clever fellow who had stolen a march on him while he was attempting to smooth over Catherine and Court's relationship. He had had to be constantly vigilant when courting Allison and Lady Janice, and still he had lost them. He should never have agreed to a friendship with Margaret. With no commitment on his part, she was free to see whomever she pleased.

"Well, perhaps calling isn't the right word," Mrs. Munroe hedged. "She is out, certainly. I'm not sure when she will return."

It was worse than he thought. Like Allison, she was probably on her way to Gretna Green with some strapping laborer with more passion than Thomas had dared show. He grit his teeth.

"I don't suppose you'd be so kind as to give me her direction?"

The woman squirmed. "I really cannot, my lord. That is, I wish you would not press me."

Thomas frowned at her.

She wilted. "Oh, please do not look at me so, my lord! It really isn't so very reprehensible. I've tried to encourage her to use her talents elsewhere, but she just won't listen."

Thomas could feel his alarm growing. "Mrs. Munroe, I came here today to ask your husband's permission to court your step-daughter. If you have information that would make me change my mind about this request, pray tell me now and spare me further humiliation."

There were tears in the woman's eyes. "Oh, my lord, please forgive her. You have every right to know. Perhaps if you marry her, you can curb these wild tendencies of hers."

"Where is she?" Thomas demanded.

Mrs. Munroe sucked back a sob. "Margaret is in the city, doing charity."

Ten

Margaret may have been doing charity, but at the moment she was feeling far from charitable. She had truly thought that spending the day at Comfort House, assisting Annie Turner (once known as the Divine Angelica), would take her mind off the Marquis DeGuis. Working at Comfort House was at best uplifting and at worst diverting. Many of the women there had opinions as strong as her own, if often entirely different. And there was always a certain pride when a young lady was brought in renouncing her vocation.

But even the fact that a new young lady was working in the kitchen instead of plying her trade in Covent Garden did not seem to raise Margaret out of the doldrums. It had been four days since their ride. Four days with no word from him. She had never been one to insist a fellow dance attendance, but she knew that if the marquis had been courting her in earnest, he would not have let so much time pass. She had followed his other courtships carefully, and he had been in almost daily communication with the ladies. Between the race and her response to his aunt, she had clearly alienated him.

Reggie, of course, had other ideas. "It is love, plain and simple," he had maintained only yesterday. "I met the marquis at White's—we are quite close, you know. He confided . . . well, perhaps I should not report what he confided. I would not wish to swell your consequence."

Margaret refused to rise to the bait. Helen was not so disciplined.

"Nephew, please," she begged, hands clasped before her. "Do not leave us in doubt. What did he say?"

Reggie watched them both, gaze darting so rapidly Margaret thought surely his eyes would cross. He leaned forward. So did her stepmother. Margaret feigned interest in the fire.

"He said," Reggie whispered as if all of London were trying to overhear, "that she is without peer."

"Oh!" Helen cried, straightening in obvious awe.

Margaret snorted. "Do not look so enraptured, madame. Is saying I am without peer not the same as saying I am an Original?"

Mrs. Munroe's face fell and she slumped.

Reggie interceded quickly. "No, no, Cousin, you mistake him. It was the *way* he said it, that is what is significant. He was positively impassioned. You have clearly won him over."

Now, with another day gone with no word, she was even less convinced her cousin knew what he was talking about. She had begun to think the Marquis DeGuis had passions, but she doubted he would parade them before a noted gossip like Reggie. No, he had only promised a friendship, and a friendship was all she had, if she even had that.

She tried to convince herself it was all to the good. He had some potentially dangerous flaw. Even if she could not quite believe that, she felt he would not have been happy married to her. She would have been miserable trying to conform to the image of a marchioness he and his family seemed to hold. But if she had never actually believed he was serious, why did his silence hurt so much?

She was glad that Annie had set her to read to Betsy Misenden that day. Betsy was nearly seventy years old and had plied her trade until only five years ago. Her illustrious career had purportedly included three earls, a royal duke, and the King of Prussia. Even though a rule of the house was to use given names, Betsy insisted that everyone address her as Little Egypt. If Annie wasn't careful, she was just as likely to encourage the young ladies to return to the streets as to start new lives. Margaret normally found her endlessly interesting. Today, it was difficult to sit in the hard wooden chair next to the iron bedstead in which the frail old woman was confined and attempt to read inspirational material. All she wanted to do was cry.

"Read that part about David and Bathsheba again," Betsy ordered. She blinked blue eyes now going blind from a disease she had caught from her last lover and leaned back against the thin pillow. Her thinning hair, the red tint finally fading after years of application, fanned out against the ticking.

Margaret thumbed to the second book of Samuel. She tried to interest herself in the familiar story, but as Betsy nearly always requested that particular set of verses, it was difficult to focus her attentions. She had only gotten through the first part when the woman interrupted her.

"One of the new girls said she heard you had gotten a hold of a Nob."

Margaret started and the Bible flipped shut accidentally. "How did you hear about that?"

"We may be living on the edge of society," Betsy

countered. "That doesn't mean we don't know what goes on. Who is he, your fellow? I might know him."

Margaret bit back a laugh. "You might indeed. But I'm not going to give you the chance to be sure. If he makes use of those in your profession, as most of the gentlemen seem to do, I imagine he is very circumspect. He is a very private person."

Betsy licked her lips. "Those make the best customers, deary. They don't want their vices known, so they pay well for silence. Do you like him?"

"Well enough," Margaret replied with a smile, which faded as she remembered his silence. "Although I suppose that doesn't matter. He appears to have decided he doesn't much like me."

Betsy sighed gustily. "Men can be like that, lovey. What's in vogue one minute is avoided the next. But there's always another fellow who's just as interested. I still think you should consider the profession. You could make a fortune with that bosom of yours."

This time Margaret did laugh. "Thank you for the compliment, I'm sure. I'll remember that if I'm ever in need."

"You'll do nothing of the sort," Annie proclaimed in the doorway, large hands on ample hips. "You stop putting such notions in her head, Betsy Misenden. She's here to help us, not to join us."

Betsy grunted and turned her worn face away from the doorway in dismissal. Annie jerked her head for Margaret to follow her into the corridor. Margaret set down the Bible on the chair and complied.

"You," Annie proclaimed accusingly, brown eyes narrowed, "have a visitor."

Margaret frowned. "A visitor? Do you mean a gentleman? I thought my friends wanted to remain anonymous."

"So did I," Annie grumbled, leading her down the

upstairs corridor in the narrow, dark little house. Her bulk, which should have looked appropriately motherly for her place as manager of the house, instead swayed with grace and seduction long practiced. "You promised none of them would come hunting here. That's the only reason I agreed to take their money. Now this fellow comes along. Riding in a carriage so shiny white dust wouldn't stick to it. Dressed in his fine clothes. Nose in the air as if he smelled something bad. He looks none too comfortable to be here, which tells me he's either innocent as a lamb or guilty as sin."

It couldn't be the marquis, Margaret told herself. He didn't know about Comfort House, and if he did, he certainly wouldn't visit it. Her heart did not appear to agree with her, for it started beating faster. Surely it was Kevin Whattling, come to see that she was using his investment wisely. "Blond haired or raven?" she asked innocently.

"Hoo-hoo, do we know so many fine gentlemen?" Annie jibed. "His hair is blacker than midnight. What I want to know is, does he have a soul to match?"

Margaret shook her head, gripping the stair rail as they descended to keep her hands from trembling. "If he's who I think he is, I would say he probably has one of the whitest souls in England."

"Does he now?" Annie mused ahead of her, her tone clearly portraying her doubt. "How well do you know him?"

"Well enough," Margaret answered. "You need have no fear of him, Annie. He's not the type to tempt your doves."

"He's a temptation just by being here," Annie insisted. "What gel in this house wouldn't go for such a fellow? Kind on the eyes, and a diamond in his cravat. Even Betsy'd find a way to climb out of that bed. I shut him up in the parlor. Send him on his way as quickly as possible. I'll keep the girls out of sight."

Margaret nodded, reaching the bottom of the stairs and going to the pocket door that closed the little parlor off from the small entryway. She still could not believe that the marquis stood behind the door. But the only other gentleman of her acquaintance with raven hair was Leslie Petersborough, and while handsome enough, he was not rich enough to be a major temptation to the ladies of Comfort House.

She slid open the door to the sparsely furnished room. Thomas turned from the fireplace as she did so. She caught her breath and halted. His face did indeed look tense, but it lightened as he realized it was her. She forced herself to let her breath out slowly and moved into the room, sliding the door shut behind her.

"My lord, what a surprise to see you again."

He bowed, straightening hastily. "A surprise, Miss Munroe? But surely you knew I would call again. I'm sorry I couldn't come to you sooner. Family matters prevented it."

"Family matters in the form of your aunt's report of our visit, I'm sure," Margaret replied with a sigh. "She was less than encouraging."

"On the contrary," he insisted. "She found you delightful."

Margaret was very tempted to call him a liar, but his earnest face told her he at least thought he was telling the truth. "She did not appear very delighted when she left," she told him.

Thomas smiled. "My aunt is a very opinionated, very stubborn woman. She respects people with equal strength of purpose."

Margaret found herself smiling. "Which means she finds me equally opinionated and stubborn. Very well. Like can recognize like."

"My sister also enjoyed your company, if that is any solace," he continued. "And she is far more difficult to draw out. However, while I value their opinions, I keep my own council. I fully intended to further our acquaintance, before their visit, and after it."

Margaret felt her face heating in a blush. "I see."

He cocked his head. "You don't sound as if you believe me. Your stepmother seemed to be under a similar impression. She seemed to find it necessary to apologize profusely."

Remembering how concerned about the race and visit her stepmother had been, Margaret could well imagine how she might have groveled. A marquis with a flaw was better than no husband at all. The thought was quite embarrassing. "I'm sorry you were subjected to that, my lord."

"On the contrary, it only made me more aware that I was being negligent. I insisted that she give me your location so that I might apologize to you immediately."

"No apology necessary," Margaret managed. "It isn't as if we are actually courting."

He stepped forward and took her hand, bringing it to his lips and nearly sending her to her knees. "That is a fact that can be remedied."

For the first time in her life she thought she might actually faint. His eyes were warm and gentle, the blue so deep she thought she might float in the depths. His smile was tender and close enough that if he moved a little closer, their lips would meet. She swallowed, willing him to kiss her, the desire stronger than anything she had ever known.

The door to the parlor slammed open.

"I knew it!" a bear of a man thundered. "I knew this was a whore house! What have you done with my Lily?"

Thomas pulled the astonished Margaret behind him, shielding her from the man's fury. Heart pounding, Margaret peered over Thomas' shoulder. Before them, chest heaving, stood a man easily over six feet tall, heavily built and shabbily dressed. His grizzled face was dark, his nose crooked as if it had been broken more than once, and his eyes bloodshot and narrowed. His meaty hands were balled in fists at his sides.

"You are mistaken, fellow," Thomas replied evenly. Margaret marveled that he could remain so calm in the face of such mountainous intimidation. "This is a home for widows and orphans. If your Lily is here, I'm sure she'd be happy to see you home."

"That she will not," Annie declared from the entryway. The fellow whirled to face her, arms swinging. Annie ducked neatly under the intended blow, stepping back out of range. "I've told you before, Jacob Breely, the likes of you are not welcome here. Lily has chosen a better way. She no longer needs a fancy man."

He eyed Thomas over his shoulder. "And what about him, then? Seems to me she's just exchanged one fancy man for another."

Margaret swallowed, realizing Annie had been right about the danger Thomas posed to the house. Annie glared at Thomas around the fellow. "He was just leaving."

"We were both leaving," Margaret amended hurriedly. She stepped boldly around Thomas, head high, insides quaking. Annie had told her about how the male solicitors often came after their girls. There wasn't a one Annie could not handle. The girls still spoke in reverent tones of the time Annie had taken a heated flat iron to the fancy man who had dared demand the return of one of her girls. The best for all concerned was if Margaret got Thomas out of here.

"Won't you see me home, my lord?" she tried.

Thomas moved to join her, but the bruising fellow would have none of it. He grabbed Margaret by the arm and hauled her up against him. She was close enough that she could see little black specks swarming over what remained of his teeth.

"And maybe I'm the one to see you home," he growled. "One girl is just as good as the next one. If that chest is real, we could do some fine business."

"Unhand her," Thomas said quietly. "Now."

The fellow had the audacity to laugh. His fetid breath washed over Margaret, and she leaned away from the noxious odor. Feeling her movement, his hand tightened on her dress and there was the unmistakable sound of tearing fabric.

Something flashed past Margaret's face and the villain stumbled backward. Blood spurted from his nose, and he let her go. Gathering her wits, Margaret scampered out of his reach. Thomas stepped forward, fists held in front of him, and smashed a right into the fellow's jaw. He blinked, swaying on his feet, then fell over backward. The house shook as his body struck the floor.

"Oh, fine," Annie complained, hands once more on hips. "What am I to do with him now?"

"I suggest," Thomas replied coldly, "that you put him out in the gutter with the rest of the trash."

Annie's dark face split in a grin. "Right you are, gov'nor. And I'll not worry each time his head bumps down a step."

Margaret ran to Thomas and threw her arms

around him. "Oh, Thomas, that was famous! You saved my life." Belatedly, she realized she had used his given name. Even worse, she was hugging him in full view of Annie and the other girls, who had appeared in the corridor now that the danger was over. Beside them stood a man with a horse whip, obviously Thomas' groom come to his aid. Even if she hadn't seen their gamin grins from the corner of her eye, she would have felt the stiffness in his body. She hastily let go of him, coloring.

Thomas' face was emotionless. "I think it is time that we leave, Miss Munroe."

Margaret swallowed. "Yes, of course. Annie, if you're sure you'll be all right."

Annie nodded, eyes narrowing once more. "We'll be fine. Though I thank your fellow for the help."

Thomas inclined his head, but he did not look at the woman as he stalked to the door, the groom dashing before him to throw it open. Margaret collected her cloak off the hall table and scurried after him. All the times she had watched him, she had thought she'd seen the range of his emotions. She'd seen him exuberant after winning a horse race and depressed after being rejected by Lady Janice. It dawned on her that this was the first time she had ever seen him angry.

Eleven

Thomas sat with back straight in his carriage. His rap on the ceiling to signal his driver to start was sharp enough to remind him of his bruised knuckles inside the gray kidskin gloves.

"Would you care to explain what that was all about?" he demanded of the woman sitting opposite him.

Margaret shrunk in on herself, wrapping her green wool cloak about her even though the day was warm enough that she should not need it. It only reminded him that beneath the cloak her lilac-sprigged muslin gown was ripped across the shoulder, her bosom speckled with the blood from the miscreant's nose. The thought of that brute laying his hands on her filled him with fury again, and he closed his eyes against the murderous anger.

"It was my stepmother who claimed it was a home for widows and orphans, wasn't it?" she asked with a sigh.

Thomas took a deep breath and opened his eyes. "Yes, although it required considerable prying to get that out of her. She seemed rather ashamed of the fact."

She sighed again. "My stepmother is entirely ashamed of my work at Comfort House. It is not a home for widows and orphans, although many of the women are both. Comfort House, my lord, is for prostitutes who have given up their profession."

He had hoped the brute was demented, even when he'd seen what appeared to be an entire host of fallen women staring through the open door. Now the man's ranting made sense.

"I see," he managed, although in truth he did not see at all. Calling this dangerous activity charity was going too far. Perhaps Court had been right that something must be done to make the streets safer. What kind of mother, or father for that matter, let a daughter consort with such people? Not only was the place unwholesome, but, if today was any indication, it was dangerous as well. If he had not been there, she might have been killed or forced against her will. The very idea made him ill. His frustration must have shown on his face, for she stiffened.

"You can let me off at the next corner, if you'd like," she said with a sniff. "I'm quite used to finding my own way home, as my stepmother refuses to allow the carriage in this neighborhood."

Looking at the brown-stone hovels they were passing, trash crowding the narrow streets, sewage running in rivets along the gutters, he could well imagine Mrs. Munroe's reluctance. He also could not imagine abandoning Margaret there. "Certainly not. I'm taking you home."

"Well, you needn't be so angry about it," she complained. "I do not agree with you or my stepmother that my work here is so reprehensible. There is a need here. These women must have a champion. They cannot return to society without one; they don't understand the rules."

"And you have proven you have little regard for the rules," he told her, unable to still his anger as

she insisted on defending the very people who had
put her in danger in the first place.

"I may have little regard for the social dictates,"
she countered, "but that doesn't mean I don't know
what the dictates are. These women need to learn a
trade, an acceptable trade, or marry, or they will have
no choice but to return to the streets. That choice is
no different than what a respectable young lady
faces."

"The two situations cannot be compared," he insisted.

She scowled at him. "Why are you so angry? Our
Lord Jesus ate with prostitutes!"

"And he had twelve able bodied men to protect
him," Thomas snapped.

"Well, if I could find twelve helpers, I assure you
I'd make use of them!"

They glared at each other for a moment, and he
felt compelled to turn his gaze to the window. Could
she not see she might have been hurt? If anything
had happened to her, he wasn't sure what he'd have
done. This need to protect her surely came from his
sense of chivalry, but this panic at the thought of
losing her was something else. The depth of it
amazed him and seemed only to fuel the anger.

She could not seem to accept his belligerence.
"Oh, come now, my lord," she put in. "I cannot believe you are one of those who pretends there is no
dark side to London. These women have been used
and abandoned by men of our own class. While you
may not be one of them, I'll wager you've had your
share of mistresses."

This time she did shock him. He whipped to face
her. "Then you would lose," he told her sternly. "I
am one of those who believes that some things should
be saved for marriage."

She stared at him. "You mean you're a virgin?"

Try as he might, he could not stop his face from flaming. "That, Miss Munroe, is none of your affair until the day we marry, a day that is looking far more unlikely every minute."

She raised her head defiantly, although he would have had to be blind not to see the hurt in her eyes. "Is that supposed to be a threat? You cannot intimidate me, my lord. Others may see you as some sort of prize that must be won at all costs, but to me you are simply a man. I never actually thought you would marry me. I do not see why you mention it now."

"Frankly, neither do I," he replied with the honesty he had come to expect of her. "I have been teased, tread upon, and tortured with encroaching questions. Why I persist is beyond me."

"There," she proclaimed, "we are in agreement at last. We will not possibly suit. You cannot court someone like me."

"Is that a challenge?"

She shrugged. "You may consider it so if you like. It is also a fact that cannot be changed. I will not be something other than what you see, my lord. You cannot be something that you disdain. It is surely better that we part, before someone gets hurt."

He curled and uncurled his fist, knuckles protesting. He had already been hurt, but he was beginning to think the pain went deeper than his sore hand. She was impossible—headstrong, impulsive, emotional—the opposite of everything he had wanted in his marchioness. Surely she was right that they break off this entanglement before it went any further. Yet the idea was repulsive to him. She had awoken something inside of him that didn't want to go back to sleep. As carefully as he had built the shell around his heart, she had cracked it.

She had grown silent, watching him with her clear blue eyes, moist now as if she were fighting tears. Had she come to care for him in so short a time? He could not imagine she even found him companionable. In her presence, his propriety felt like stuffiness, his honor merely the following of unarticulated social dictates. Surely she could not even like him. Something in him burned to know the answer.

"Tell me, Miss Munroe, would you want me to court you?"

She turned her gaze to the window. "That is the third time someone has asked me something like that, my lord. One was a close friend, the other was your aunt. If I did not see fit to answer them, I do not see why I should answer you."

He sighed. "Must you be so prickly? Is there nothing of import we can discuss without disagreeing?"

"It would appear not. But let's by all means be fair about this. Tell me, my lord the marquis, would you want to court me, knowing me as you do now?"

The challenge was there, clearly set before him, just as on the day she had challenged him to race. Then as now, he argued with himself, brought all his logic to bear, debated as sincerely as if he were on the floor of Parliament, battling for a favorite bill. She was nothing like the woman he thought he wanted. But perhaps what he wanted and what he needed were two different things. In the end, he lost, and he won.

"Yes, Miss Munroe," he replied sincerely. "I would like to court you."

She did not turn her gaze from the window, but he thought she shivered. "Very well, my lord. But do not expect miracles. I am what I am."

"Agreed. I will try to stop being judgmental. But

as you said, we should be fair. Am I not allowed to be what I am?"

She started, turning to him at last, eyes wide. "Good heavens, I have been judging you, haven't I? I sincerely apologize, my lord. Of course, you must be yourself. As that is practically perfect, I don't know why I would want to change you."

Her praise should have warmed him, but it only served to remind him of his gaping failure in his last two courtships. He had sincerely cared for Allison. He had admired Lady Janice. He was beginning to think that Margaret Munroe would settle for nothing short of an impassioned love. That was the one thing he could not give her. This time he was the one to turn away.

"I am not perfect, Miss Munroe. Seeing me that way is in itself a form of judgment. I find I prefer your statement that I am merely a man."

"But such a man," she teased. "Haven't I heard the phrase, catch of the season? My stepmother utters it often enough."

He wanted to smile, but somehow could not manage it. "I think we may also agree that your stepmother is perhaps blinded by the title and the estates that go with it."

"As is every other match-making mama of the ton," Margaret insisted. She was quiet for a moment. When she spoke again, her tone was much gentler. "Is something troubling you, my lord? You will remember I told you I preferred we be honest in all things. If something about courting me concerns you, please let us discuss it."

He quirked a wry smile. "Why, what could possibly concern me about a courtship we both agree is madness?"

She smiled in return. "Everything. And nothing.

If we are mad, perhaps we will cease to notice the difficulties."

"Perhaps," he allowed.

Her smile faded, and she bit her lip. He felt himself stiffen. "Am I being unfair again? Is there something about this courtship that troubles *you*, Miss Munroe, aside from the fact that we are both mad?"

It was the only time he had seen her hesitate, and somehow it chilled him. "A person I would normally consider well-meaning tells me that I should refuse to be seen with you. She says she and my cousin Allison know something about you that would make me afraid to be your wife."

It was another challenge, but one he could not meet, not with the honesty she wanted. The person who had spoken to her could only be Lady Janice. He had not thought her so vindictive as to spread malicious gossip. But perhaps, as Margaret had noted, she thought to spare her friend heartache. This was his opportunity to confess his shortcomings to Margaret, but, as much as he wanted to continue this association, he was not ready to bare his soul to her. She may have opened his heart, but the wounds left by his last two courtships were still too raw to probe deeply. He was simply not ready to open that part of himself to pain again.

"Perhaps she was referring to my temper," he hedged. "You just received a rather marked demonstration, I'm afraid. It has a long fuse, but once it reaches the powder, the results tend to be explosive. I promise to apologize profusely afterward."

She looked doubtful, and he waited for more questions. But she did not press him. Instead, she settled back against the squabs with a pensive look. He could not be so sanguine. Knowing her as he was beginning to, he was sure the matter would resurface, probably when he least wanted it to.

Besides, he had some thinking of his own to do. It was unlike him to do something so illogical as to agree to a courtship he was ill-prepared to finish. Obviously, whatever part of him that had urged him to do so had nothing to do with logic. He felt as if he were out to sea without a compass. It would be a struggle to find familiar land again, and the same illogical part of him wasn't sure he wanted to. He had thought all he wanted was a simple marriage to continue the line. Instead, he had just agreed to a courtship that could well cost him his sanity, his character, and his heart.

It would be one amazing ride.

Twelve

Margaret would have liked nothing better than to feel in complete charity with Thomas. After all, he had overcome his righteous indignation concerning the incident at Comfort House and declared he wished to court her. She should be in alt. Instead, she found herself quite annoyed.

It did not help that he insisted on accompanying her into the house. For once, she knew, his presence would not be enough to ward off a scold from her stepmother. Indeed, she had the impression from the tight smile on Thomas' face that he took perverse delight in hearing the woman babble on about the damage to her clothes, her reputation, and her virtue, in that order. After several minutes of the diatribe, Margaret was ready to stamp from the room, leaving the marquis to the questionable graces of her stepmother. Unfortunately, Thomas must have noted the rebellion in her eyes, for he interrupted Mrs. Munroe in mid-sentence.

"I quite agree with you that Miss Munroe should be more careful in her choice of charities," he told Helen, who swallowed whatever else she was going to say to listen to him. "I'm certain today's events have taught us all a lesson, one Mr. Munroe would appreciate as well. Has he returned from his club, do you know? I would like a moment of his time."

This statement sent her stepmother into fresh agitation, but Margaret was not fooled. He had no intention of offering for her hand; he had only just agreed to court her. He was clearly set on convincing her father to keep her away from Comfort House.

"I appreciate your concern for my safety, my lord," she told him. "But I still maintain that I am in no danger. Scolding my father will not keep me from my duty."

Thomas shook his head, but the presence of Mrs. Munroe obviously had him hobbled. Margaret felt a grin forming. As a gentleman of noted composure, he could scarcely argue with her in public. As an Original, she felt no such qualms. The power was heady.

"Margaret." The word rumbled out of her stepmother in warning before the little woman turned a beaming smile on the marquis. "My lord, I regret that my husband has yet to return. Perhaps we might speak instead."

Thomas bowed. "Your servant, madame. However, I'm afraid this is a matter for the head of the house."

Margaret bit her lips to keep from laughing at the annoyance that flickered across her stepmother's round face. It was no secret who ran the Munroe household. Mrs. Munroe pasted on a smile as Thomas straightened.

"Then perhaps we should set a time of convenience for you," she tried.

Thomas smiled. "No hurry. I'll try to meet with him the next time I visit."

"And that will be?" Helen asked brightly.

Thomas affixed Margaret with a stern look. "Tomorrow at three."

"We will be home," Mrs. Munroe replied, her tone daring Margaret to disagree. Thomas bowed again and left.

"Now see what you've done!" her stepmother declared as soon as the door closed behind him. "He was ready to ask for your hand, and you spoiled it with your silly charity!"

Margaret turned to the stairs in disgust. "As he asked for Father after the incident, I do not think my 'silly charity' had any effect."

"But surely you could see how upset he was," Helen pressed, following her up the stairs. "Do not go back there, Margaret."

"I must," Margaret replied with determination. "I have a responsibility to those women. Until there are others to take my place, I will not leave Annie alone."

"Your only responsibility is to this family," Helen argued. "You cannot expect your father to support you for the rest of your life. Do you wish to remain a spinster?"

"Do you never tire of this argument?" Margaret countered, reaching the door of her room. "The marquis agreed to court me. Be happy with that."

"But Margaret," her stepmother began.

"No 'buts,' madame," Margaret interrupted. "Nothing will deter me. Now, excuse me while I change."

"You'll need to change," her stepmother muttered, but she did not follow her through the door. "If there is any hope for this courtship, you'll need to change a great deal."

Of course, she had gone in the morning to check on Annie, finding the woman in the cavernous kitchen of the house, which they had turned into a laundry.

"Safe and secure, we are," the ex-prostitute replied to her concern, though she was quick to lead Margaret back to the little parlor as the girls turned eagerly to question her. "I expect I'll see Jacob Breely again, stubborn as he is," she admitted as they were seated on the worn settee. "But he'll think twice after that crack your Nob gave him."

"Then there are no bad repercussions from Lord DeGuis' visit?" Margaret probed, concerned that she had been hurried away from the very women she was here to help.

"Bad things, you ask?" Annie's face fell easily into her regular scowl. "Well, I can't call it a blessing. Seems the girls have discussed little else since then."

"But surely they discuss any visit by someone of Jacob Breely's stripe," Margaret protested, compelled to defend Thomas and herself for causing him to come to the house.

Annie snorted, sounding very like Aeolus when he was miffed. " 'Tweren't Mr. Breely they were discussing. Seems your Nob came off quite the hero. I heard bets being laid this morning as to which of them had a better chance of catching him."

"Lord DeGuis is very handsome," Margaret agreed with a sigh. "It's little wonder they want to catch his eye."

" 'Tweren't his eye they wanted to catch," Annie muttered darkly.

Margaret felt herself blushing. "Well, he claims to have little use for your girls, Annie."

"That I well believe," Annie replied heatedly. "Why touch coppers when gold lays itself at your feet? He could have his pick of ladies, high born and low."

"Yes," Margaret said quietly. "I know."

Annie sighed heavily. "There! I swear I gave up my winning ways when I gave up the profession. Can you believe butter wouldn't have melted in my mouth once? I was that eager to please my gents. Now I've hurt your feelings, and you one of the few to help us."

"I'm fine," Margaret replied with a rueful smile. "I try to speak only the truth. Why should I mind when others do so? Lord DeGuis and I had quite a discussion yesterday about Comfort House. Much as I disagree with his points, I cannot argue that he is a paragon, Annie. I have yet to hear anyone seriously contest that, with any evidence that is."

Annie's face darkened again, and she shifted in her seat. "Well, you may yet hear something."

Margaret frowned, leaning forward. "What have you heard?"

"Not much," Annie grumbled.

When Margaret laughed at her obvious pique, she hurried to qualify the statement.

"None of the girls had ever served him. Nor had they met anyone who could make the claim. If I hadn't seen him after you, I'd start to wonder whether he liked gents better."

Margaret shook her head. "I would find that difficult to believe."

Annie cracked a grin worthy of Betsy Misenden. "That lusty, is he?"

Her face was heating again. She could have loved to lie, but could not. "Actually, he has yet to so much as kiss me," she admitted grudgingly.

"Remarkable," Annie said, grin fading. "Much as I hate to agree with Betsy, that chest of yours ought to be right tempting. He's either the coldest fish in London, or the oddest."

"I tell you he is simply a gentleman," Margaret

insisted. "After working here, I am as surprised as you are that one of his caliber still exists. I am certain that if he makes up his mind that he loves me, he will demonstrate that love to my satisfaction." *And if he doesn't,* she amended silently, *I will never agree to marry him, otherwise perfect or no.*

"Good for you," Annie replied with a nod. "I'll say no more on the matter, then, seeing as you know what you want. Just watch yourself, Miss Margaret."

Margaret reached out and squeezed Annie's roughened hands. "I will, Annie. Now, won't you please put me to work as you usually do?"

To her surprise, Annie shook her head. "Not here, I won't. Sounds like we need your help elsewhere. Did you see the story in the *Times*? The Lords are fixing to send us to workhouses."

Margaret had been teaching a number of the women to read, using the *London Times* and the Bible as her text books. Now she wondered which of the many articles Annie might have read. "Do you mean the story on the amendment to the Poor Laws?" she guessed.

"Poor Laws," Annie spit out contemptuously. "Them laws don't help the poor. But that was what the paper said."

"I saw the article as well. I won't cover it with honey, Annie. You are right that this bill could be trouble. When I first heard of it, I had Lord Petersborough get a copy of the wording from his father for me. After reading it, I admit I did not think anyone would be foolish enough to give it serious consideration. From what the *Times* said, it would appear I was wrong."

"Then they will send us to workhouses?" Despite her scowl, Annie was obviously asking her to deny it. Margaret shook her head.

"What the bill says, Annie, is that anyone who cannot claim to be practicing a legal trade or have an independent income can be sent to a workhouse."

Annie's face tightened. "I knew it! Bleedin' Tories! They'd see their own mothers in prison if it would bring in a farthing to the Crown."

"Cursing them will do us little good," Margaret cautioned, mind working. "We must make our supporters aware of the damage this bill could do to any of our charitable works. Until the girls at Comfort House have been here for at least a fortnight, they cannot claim to know anything but their former profession. It takes at least that long to convince them to stay and help them to learn the laundry. If they are to serve as laundresses to some of the better homes, they have much to learn. Someone vindictive like Jacob Breely could easily alert the authorities and have the girls carted off before we had done any good at all."

"I'll lie," Annie fumed. "I'll tell any who ask that every one of our girls is employed."

"Lying is never the answer," Margaret replied. "It will not satisfy our enemies. Nor will it show the girls the way to a better life. No, the bill must be defeated before it is enacted." She rose, determined. "Leave this to me, Annie. I will contact our supporters and urge them to accost members of Parliament on our behalf. They must be made to see how wrong this bill is."

Margaret started with Thomas that afternoon. She had to wait while he met in the withdrawing room with her father.

"Stop pacing," her stepmother, who waited with

her, ordered. "You do not want to appear flustered when he asks you to marry him."

"For the last time, madame," she told the woman, "he is *not* asking for my hand."

Helen shook her head. "Why else would he want to speak with your father? Do you think he will wait until Parliament has adjourned to have the wedding? The ton will be short of people then, but I suppose they might return for such an event."

Margaret ignored her.

A moment later, her father came out. He beamed at Margaret and patted her shoulder. "He wants to court you," he whispered with a wink. "You have him on your hook, gel. Play him out and pull him in."

Margaret shook her head at his enthusiasm, then scooted past him into the withdrawing room as he turned to explain the situation to Helen.

"Did you have to do that?" she asked as soon as Thomas had offered her a bow in welcome. He raised an eyebrow at her tone and she sighed, slumping into the chair opposite him. "Sorry. I'm more upset than I thought."

He frowned. "About my speaking to your father? I assure you, it is only a formality. You had already agreed to let me court you in earnest."

Something about his frown told her he was concerned she might have changed her mind. "You had every right to speak to my father, my lord," she assured him. "The matter that concerns me has nothing to do with our courtship." She took a deep breath and launched into her thoughts on the Poor Laws amendment. A quarter of an hour later, she became aware that he was leaning back on the sofa, smiling as if she amused him.

"This isn't a joke," she told him heatedly. "The bill leaves too much to interpretation. What is a legal trade? How many hours must one work at it to be considered 'practicing'? Further, it makes no provisions for those in apprenticeships nor those in less formal training. If this bill was stretched to extremes, half the students in Oxford could be carted off to a workhouse."

"I doubt that would happen," he interjected.

"Of course it wouldn't happen. They have highborn parents or sponsors to support them. Who will support the women of Comfort House, indeed, in any charitable institution in the country?"

Thomas clapped his hands. "Well spoken, my dear. I only wish you could take the floor of Parliament. You make an eloquent and lovely advocate."

"Oh!" Margaret huffed, glaring at him. "If you will not take me seriously, how can I expect anyone else to?"

His smile of appreciation faded. "I assure you, Miss Munroe, I take you very seriously indeed. It is obvious that you do not play at your good works as do some of the ladies of the ton. Much as I worry for your safety, I commend your devotion to the unfortunate ladies of Comfort House. I have only recently seen the bill myself, but I promise you I will bear your points in mind when I consider it."

Margaret felt her frustration melting. "Thank you, my lord. I should have known you'd approach this intelligently."

"Thank *you*," he nodded, smile returning. "And you are right to be concerned. With so many returning soldiers on the streets and Wellington's victory making excuses for endless celebration, many of my fellow peers are struggling with the apparent lawlessness of the citizenry. I have never been enamored of workhouses, but they are an easy solution."

"Then we must press for a lasting solution," Margaret maintained.

"Agreed. Would you like the opportunity to try?"

She cocked her head, eyeing him. That smile was confident, but she still was not certain he was not merely placating her. "What do you have in mind?"

He leaned forward. "I've been invited to the Prince Regent's supper celebrating the return of Wellington. Every influential member of Lords will be there, including the Prime Minister and his cabinet. I would be honored to escort you as my guest."

Margaret stared at him. Her first thought was that her stepmother would swoon at the idea of her stepdaughter mixing in such august company. Cousin Reggie would kill for such an invitation. Her second thought was that this would indeed be a perfect opportunity to impact the dreaded amendment. But when she considered the social constraints she would have to endure to achieve her goal, she could feel her palms start to sweat.

"But your sister, your aunt," she protested feebly. "Won't they expect you to escort them instead?"

"My sister abhors crowds and my aunt will want to remain with her," Thomas replied easily. Margaret could not help thinking that the quiet Lady Catherine had the right of it in this instance. But then, Lady Catherine did not have a cause to defend.

"Then I would be honored to accept, my lord," she murmured. "But are you sure you are willing to appear in such company with a noted Original on your arm?"

He rose to take her hand and bring it to his lips. As always, she trembled at his touch. "I have no doubt you will put them completely in the shade. Shall I pick you up at half past eight?"

Margaret nodded numbly. She knew she should

follow her own philosophy and seize the moment, but her heart quailed.

Even on the arm of a noted paragon like the Marquis DeGuis and for the best of causes, could the Original Miss Margaret Munroe be a social belle for even one night?

Thirteen

Thomas, of course, had no such concerns. To him, having Margaret campaign among society's leaders for the rights of fallen women was far safer than Margaret working among those women. Besides, if she was to be his marchioness, she'd have to accustom herself to an occasional state dinner. He was not numbered among the Regent's favorites, being far too conservative and quiet for Prinny's opulent tastes. However, as a peer of the realm, he was expected to exude a certain amount of pomp and ceremony. His wife would have to follow suit.

Besides, he had been impressed with her analysis of the bill's limitations. He wondered how she'd fare against the equally determined Viscount Darton. Lady Jersey and Lady Melbourne had long been known for their abilities to sway politics behind the scenes. Though by accident of birth they could not set foot on the floor of the Lords, they managed to see their agendas raised and passed. Margaret Munroe had the intelligence and drive to do no less.

He attempted to call the following day, having vowed to be more attentive now that they were courting. However, he found Margaret out shopping with her stepmother and Mr. Munroe already gone to his club. He did not have a chance to talk to Margaret until he arrived to pick her up that evening. Even then, he was forced to wait and natter about the weather and Wellington to Mr. Munroe. But he could not deny the wait was worth it. There was a step on the stair, and Mr. Munroe's face split into a smile of pride. Turning, Thomas found himself confronting the goddess of the moon.

Margaret's gown was of a blue as deep as midnight, with its own luster. It was simply cut, laying close to her creamy skin and emphasizing the curve of her generous bosom. Draped over the top and no less fitting was the lightest of blonde lace overskirts sown with beads that caught the light like stars in the night sky as she moved. Her dark hair was bound with silver, one heavy curl falling along her neck. His eyes followed to where it rested against the top of one breast. For a fleeting second, he wondered what it would be like to rest his lips on the same spot. Heat rushed to his face as well as other portions of his anatomy, and he bowed deeply to hide his surprise at the reaction.

"Miss Munroe, I am the most blest of mortals," he proclaimed as he straightened. "What other gentleman may claim to be escorting a goddess?"

"Diana," her father put in with a chuckle. "Didn't I say so when you described the dress to me?"

She had not moved from the top of the stair, as frozen in her regard of him as he had been in his regard of her. He was not sure what arrested her. His valet had insisted he wear something more festive than his usual evening black, and he had been surprised to learn he owned a coat of cobalt blue with gold buttons. He was even more surprised to find he owned a sapphire waistcoat heavily embroidered with gold.

"A gift from your sister," Jimms had explained when Thomas had asked.

Now by Margaret's mesmerized look, he was glad he'd followed the fellow's advice. Unfortunately, if she didn't stop staring, he was going to be put to the blush again.

Luckily, she shook herself and moved gracefully down the stairs, her skirt trailing regally behind. "Good evening, my lord," she murmured as Thomas brought her gloved hand to his lips.

"Wait, wait," Mrs. Munroe panted, nearly throwing herself down the stairs. "You forgot your ear bobs."

Margaret made a face as the woman hurried to her side. "Oh, must I wear them? They pinch."

"Hush," Mrs. Munroe chided, then, obviously catching Thomas' gaze on her, she colored. "I'm sure the marquis will appreciate how they compliment your gown."

Thomas had the feeling this was the last in a long series of arguments, many of which Margaret had lost. "What need to improve on perfection?" he quipped, earning him a glowing smile from the lady.

Mrs. Munroe was gaping. She reminded him suddenly of Pinstin; apparently the fish imitation ran in the family. Bidding the Munroes good night, Thomas offered Margaret his arm and swept her from the house.

"Will she forgive me by the time we return?" he joked after they were seated in the carriage and heading toward Carleton House.

"Much sooner than that," Margaret promised him. "You will notice I have been sent with no chaperone."

Thomas frowned. "It is only a short distance to Carleton House. Surely I can be trusted to behave like a gentleman for that long."

Her eyes twinkled in the lamplight. "And if not,

surely you will be enough of a gentleman to rectify matters."

"She would wish you compromised?" He could see he was going to have to work tonight to keep from being shocked or embarrassed.

"She would never wish anything bad to happen to me," Margaret assured him. "But I have come to realize we have different definitions of the word 'bad.' "

"Nonetheless," he replied earnestly, "I hope you know you are safe with me."

She cast him a quick look, then turned her gaze to the window. "I have never doubted that, my lord," she murmured.

It was indeed only a short while before his driver was slowing for the traffic before the Prince Regent's London residence. Margaret peered out the window, wide-eyed.

"Quite a crush," he remarked with a smile at her amazement.

She turned an awed face in his direction. "Everyone in London must be here."

"Oh, no," he assured her as they took their place in the queue of countless carriages. "Only a few thousand of the regent's closest friends."

When the carriage finally stopped, Thomas waved away the liveried, bewigged footman and handed Margaret down himself. She looked no less awed at the candlelight blazing from the windows of the classical mansion. As they walked arm-in-arm through the soaring columns that marked the entrance, she had her head tipped so far back to see the frescoes on the pediments that he thought the rest of her hair would fall. A passing matron raised an eyebrow but the look Thomas returned caused her to urge her escort ahead.

More footmen directed them through the house, although, Thomas reflected, they had only to follow the crowds. Margaret blinked again as they stepped into a round hall, easily one hundred and forty feet in diameter. The walls were draped with white muslin and the roof was painted a dull white to match. A Grecian temple in the center was surrounded by silk flowers. By the gentle rhythms emanating from it, he would guess it had been designed to hide the musicians who were playing for over a hundred couples. It was a sign of Margaret's amazement that she did not immediately clamor to join them.

"This is Nash's work, I'll wager," he told her, thinking of the flamboyant architect the regent had brought into prominence. A passing servant offered champagne, which Thomas accepted for himself and Margaret. She took the gilt-edged crystal flute, but her gaze continued to dart among the bejeweled, satin-gowned ladies and velvet-coated gentlemen like a hummingbird among a garden of flowers.

"It is most impressive," she managed.

Thomas nodded to several acquaintances, his own gaze roaming for Court, who would be a good choice to discuss Margaret's bill. Among the press, he did not spy the viscount easily. Tucking Margaret's hand in his elbow, he guided her through the crowd, stopping here and there to make introductions and exchange pleasantries. They made their way through the receiving line, greeting the prince, several military leaders, and finally Wellington himself.

"He must be a better general than a statesman," Margaret commented as they moved back into the promenading couples. "That long hawkish nose might be considered impressive, but his mouth is far too expressive. He seems to be either amused or dismayed by this honor."

"He is not one for ostentation," Thomas acknowledged, appreciating her quick assessment. He led her back through the crowd, searching for a likely lord. Even though he knew she had a goal in mind, he could see her gaze moving more and more toward the dancers. If he did not find her a debate partner soon, she was likely to succumb to her favorite pastime.

Halfway around the hall he spied Lord Malcolm Breckonridge, leader of the moderate Whigs, and moved in to introduce Margaret to him. He had wondered whether he would have to help steer the conversation onto the amendment, but she proved her usual direct self.

"And how do you plan to vote on the Poor Law amendment, my lord?" she asked as soon as the fellow had straightened from his bow.

Thomas watched as Breckonridge raised a craggy black eyebrow. A tall, powerfully built fellow with unkempt raven hair and rugged features, he had cultivated a reputation for intimidation, physically and intellectually. Margaret remained undaunted, a fact that clearly impressed him.

"The bill would appear to be timely," he allowed. "But I'm not sure how effective it would be at solving the problem."

Thomas hid a smile at the carefully worded statement. Margaret immediately set out to convince him of the bill's many flaws. A half hour later, she had gathered a crowd of two earls, a duke, five members of the Commons, and seven assorted ministers. He watched her argue passionately while around her, his fellow Parliamentarians nodded and questioned and jostled each other to get in on the debate. He stepped aside to let another eager lord through and found Lady Sally Jersey at his side.

"That's certainly the first time Miss Munroe has ever drawn such a following," she remarked with her typical waspish humor.

"Even the jaded ton can recognize sincerity," he replied as Lord Breckonridge chuckled at something Margaret had said. He didn't think he'd ever seen the man laugh before.

"So can I," Lady Jersey told him. "Let Miss Munroe know she has other supporters, from a constituency less visible, but no less powerful."

Thomas raised her hand to his lips. "I thank you for the lady."

Her eyes smiled at him before she strolled away.

The interest in Margaret's expostulation did not wane until supper was called. Then Thomas had to elbow his way to her side to prevent one of the other gentlemen from claiming her as a partner. Her color was high and her blue eyes were bright, but he doubted she had taken more than a sip from the champagne she still held.

"A triumph, my dear," he proclaimed as he led her down one of the covered walks to a tent set up in the gardens. There were several such tents, each lined with transparent murals through which candlelight glowed. The mural on their tent seemed to have something to do with the defeat of Napoleon, but the neoclassical figures were so overdrawn he could not be sure. As he turned to locate a pair of seats, he was pleased to find Court winding his way toward him and held up Margaret to wait.

"I saw you earlier," Court explained after a stiff bow toward Margaret. "But could not reach you through the crowd. Was it Lord Wellington?"

"Not Wellington," Thomas replied with a smile toward Margaret. "But someone equally capable of commanding attention. I believe the ton has christened a new Incomparable."

"Nonsense, my lord," she answered, sharing his smile. "There is simply a class of gentlemen who enjoy a good debate. I do not doubt that tomorrow I shall find myself once more merely an Original."

"We should find seats," Court interjected, nodding to where the supper tables were rapidly filling.

Thomas led Margaret to a nearby table and sat beside her. Court attempted to sit beside him, but a cavalry officer beat him to the chair. Court bowed and went to sit on the other side of Margaret instead. Thomas could hardly fail to notice the tight set to the viscount's mouth. He found it difficult to credit that his friend still held a grudge against Margaret for beating him in a race, but then the viscount was not known for losing gracefully. Since he so rarely lost, his fits of pique were easily forgotten. He wondered whether it would be advisable to leave them alone, but when he rose to fill their gold plates from the buffet, Court went with him. He had no time to converse with his friend, however, as the press of the crowd prevented intimate conversation.

Despite her popularity, Margaret had obviously not lost touch with her goal in attending the fete. No sooner had Thomas brought her her supper than she turned to Court. "And what do you think of the Poor Law amendment, my lord?"

Court eyed her, then slid a glance at Thomas beyond her as if unsure how forthright he was supposed to be.

"Viscount Darton helped pen the bill," Thomas put in, hoping he wasn't starting another war Wellington would have to finish. "Go ahead, Court. Miss Munroe would benefit from hearing someone defend the amendment."

"I take it you have heard something about the bill that distresses you?" the viscount asked Margaret. "You need not worry, Miss Munroe. This bill will do nothing but help the poor."

"On the contrary," Margaret declared, eyes flashing like lightning from a darkening sky. "This bill will do nothing but hurt the poor."

"You are opposed to workhouses, I suppose," Court replied, sparing Thomas a glance that said he thought Thomas had originated the idea. Thomas shook his head, but Court had already returned his attention to Margaret.

"I find them totally reprehensible," she was saying. "The Church of England and a host of high-minded citizens have developed a number of practices that lead to rehabilitation for those who have no legal vocation. This bill would undermine everything they have worked to achieve."

"And those same citizens complain of the high cost of the Poor Rates they pay," Court countered. "This bill will allow us to cut those taxes in half."

"But at what cost?" she persisted. "Women and children forced to labor. Families separated. You ask too much, Lord Darton."

"I fear you view this entirely too emotionally, Miss Munroe," the viscount chided. Thomas shook his head again to warn the viscount he was moving onto shaky ground, but apparently Darton did not see him. "Governance," he continued, "is not for the tender-hearted."

"Nor for the weak-minded," Margaret snapped.

Court stiffened even as Thomas rolled his eyes at the insult. "Then it is a very good thing you cannot vote on this issue, Miss Munroe," he said before pointedly turning away from her to engage the fellow on his left in conversation.

"Was that last shot necessary?" Thomas murmured, drawing her attention away from his friend. Her eyes still snapped fire and her mouth was a thin line of annoyance.

"I will not apologize," she declared. "To you or to him. How dare he placate me! He never could stand to be bested, especially by a woman. If you ask me, that points to an overly inflated sense of self-worth."

"Or lack of confidence," Thomas pointed out gently. "He's still young. Give him a few more years and he will yet turn into a noted statesman."

"If he continues this way, he won't live long enough," she muttered darkly. "Someone besides me will surely be upset enough to call him out."

Thomas raised an eyebrow at her vehemence. While he thought he had gotten used to her passionate nature, he was surprised to find that she was as firm in her own grudges as she was in her admirations. He wondered just where he stood along the spectrum and was more than a little afraid to find out. But somehow he knew she'd be only too pleased to tell him, if his guarded heart would lend him the courage to ask.

Fourteen

Margaret was not sure whether to cheer or collapse in a dead faint. There could no longer be any question that the Marquis DeGuis was serious in his courtship. Since the celebration for Wellington, he had called every day. Sometimes they rode, other times they drove out into the country. He escorted her to the opera and the theater. He came personally to tell her that the Poor Laws amendment would not reach the floor before Parliament recessed for the end of the summer, bringing her flowers to celebrate her victory and listening with a smile to her cheers. He had accepted her challenge race each of the six times she had offered it. Although he had yet to waltz with her, one could not have asked for a more attentive, considerate suitor. Her stepmother was beside herself in delight.

He was the perfect gentleman, although Margaret could not quite forget his behavior at Comfort House and their conversation afterward. It could easily be that it was his temper that had frightened away Lady Janice and Allison. She would never have suspected such white hot fury could exist in so otherwise calm a gentleman. Neither did she feel he would ever turn that temper on anyone he loved. However, as she still had no word from her cousin, she could not be certain.

Even more amazing was the day less than a fortnight from their agreement that he came to call on her father. She did not even know he had been there until her father wandered into the sewing room at the back of the house, where Margaret and Helen were want to work together. That day she was helping her stepmother replace a worn collar on one of her winter dresses. She looked up and smiled as her father came into the room. He winked at her, then went to plant a kiss on his wife's bowed head. Mrs. Munroe looked up in surprise.

"Goodness, what was that for?" she exclaimed, needle frozen in mid-stitch.

"For shepherding the most clever girl in London," her father replied cheerfully.

Margaret's smile deepened, but her stepmother frowned. "You are forever saying that about Margaret. I quite agree with you that she is clever. What has suddenly brought it to your attention again today?"

"My visitor this morning. He was quite insistent on her many fine qualities."

Her stepmother continued to frown, but Margaret felt her heart jump. "Who was visiting this morning, Father?"

"Who indeed?" Her father chuckled, obviously enjoying the fact that for once he knew more than they did. "A fine fellow, if I'm not mistaken. Tall, imposing, titled."

Mrs. Munroe clutched the needle. "The Marquis DeGuis? Has he come up to scratch?"

Margaret rose shakily to her feet. "I do not believe it. He wouldn't be so old-fashioned as to ask you before he asked me."

"Now, now, of course not," her father soothed. "Though I must say it did my heart good to hear him praise you so. Let's see, how did that go? Honest, intelligent, witty, willing to live for her principles. Now, that's the daughter I raised."

"Do stop prattling," her stepmother ordered. "What did he say? Is he going to marry Margaret?"

"And don't you want to know about his qualifications before I answer that question?" her father challenged.

Margaret knew all about his qualifications, primary of which was the fact that despite any character flaw she was still helplessly in love with him. Her stepmother was even less willing to wait.

"I know his qualifications," she replied with a sniff. "He is rich, titled, and a gentleman. What did he say?"

"There is more to the fellow than that," her father insisted. "For one thing, he rides. And he rides well. Did you know he's won eighteen of the twenty races he's entered?"

"Yes," Margaret answered with a smile.

"That is hardly important," Mrs. Munroe protested.

"Furthermore, he tithes ten percent of his annual income to the Church of England, and another ten percent to worthy charities."

"Really?" Margaret mused, thinking of all the good she might do Comfort House with that kind of funding. She put the thought hastily away. She would likely never be his wife, and it was greedy to think how she might spend someone else's money.

"That is quite commendable, I'm sure," her stepmother said. "Now, get to the point, if you please. Did you or did you not give him permission to marry Margaret?"

"I did not," her father replied.

Margaret sank back onto the chair, heart dropping to the soles of her feet. "You didn't?"

"You didn't?" Helen gasped, collapsing against the back of her own chair.

"I didn't," her father echoed. He winked at Margaret again. "The fellow admitted he does not waltz. I told him to take lessons."

Margaret felt a laugh bubbling up. "Oh, Father, you didn't."

"Oh, Marcus, you didn't!" her stepmother cried, straightening again with fire in her eyes.

"I most certainly did," her father countered. "I told him he has permission to marry my daughter as soon as he can acquit himself well on the dance floor, or whenever my daughter informs me that she is willing to have him."

Margaret sprung from the chair and threw her arms about him. "Oh, Father, thank you!"

"Well, I must say, you took long enough to get around to it." Helen sighed. But she too rose and enfolded them both in a hug. "Our lives are made, my dears. Margaret, I'm so happy for you."

Margaret chuckled, disengaging. "Do not crow yet. He hasn't actually asked me."

"Oh, but he shall," Mrs. Munroe predicted. "I can feel it. You will be Lady Thomas DeGuis before the end of the year, mark my words."

"Sooner than that, perhaps," her father remarked with a chuckle. "We're invited to spend two months at his estate in the Lake District."

"Really?" her stepmother asked with a frown.

"Really," her father insisted. "And I am getting quite tired of no one believing what I say. You stand there and argue and our Margaret looks none too pleased. I thought you'd enjoy the visit, my dear.

You've always said you thought that part of the country sounded heavenly."

Margaret nodded absently. In truth, everything she had heard about the area, the sparkling blue lakes, the vibrant green hillsides, the towering crags, sounded beautiful beyond words. But in so quiet a setting, wouldn't the differences between her and the marquis be all the more noticeable? She would probably have no doubts as to his character, and the flaws therein, or his feelings by the end of that time. Somehow the thought concerned her.

"Give her time to get used to the idea," her stepmother counseled. "I'm sure she'll be delighted. When do we leave?"

"At the end of the fortnight," her father replied.

Mrs. Munroe sighed deeply. "Summer in the country. It's been ages since I've had a chance. Margaret, promise me you will do nothing to anger the marquis in the next fortnight. I simply couldn't bear it if this trip were canceled."

Margaret smiled woodenly. "Certainly, madame. I'll be my usual charming self."

"That's all anyone can ask." Her father said with a nod. Her stepmother frowned, but wisely said nothing. Instead, she hurried from the room muttering about packing.

Others had varying reactions to the news that Margaret was to spend two months in the country with the Marquis DeGuis.

"And how are we supposed to get on without you?" Annie Turner demanded when Margaret told her the next day. "What if another cove shows up?"

"You've told me repeatedly that you can handle things," Margaret reminded her. "Besides, it was the marquis who quelled the last fellow, not me. You know that law you were worried about will not come

to pass until next spring at the earliest, and I promise
to keep campaigning as soon as everyone returns
from the summer recess. Is there anything else you
need me for?"

Annie tried to look defiant, then her sagging face
dropped even further and she threw her arms about
Margaret. "I'll miss you, girl! Don't you let that fellow
lay a hand on you, you hear? You hold out for a gold-
en band."

Margaret hugged her back. "Do not trouble yourself on that score. I never intended to settle for anything less. If the man marries me, it will be because
he loves me."

Her cousin Reginald, of course, had other ideas.

"Hillwater," he enthused, beady eyes bright. "Only
his intimates get invited there. When do we leave?"

"In less than a fortnight," her stepmother answered, apparently not noticing Reggie's inclusion of
himself in the matter. Margaret was not so easily
swayed.

" 'We' are not leaving at all," she informed him.
"You weren't included in the invitation, Reggie."

He drew himself up to his full height, barely looking her in the eye, and raised his quizzing glass. Margaret glared at him and he hastily dropped the thing.
"Am I not part of this family?" he whined with
wounded dignity. "Naturally, I assumed I would be
included in the party."

"In truth, I did not think to ask your father how
many were invited," Helen put in with a frown. "Perhaps we should consult the marquis. I'm sure he
would not want to leave anyone out."

Reggie preened. "And he is a great friend of mine.
I'm certain he would want me along."

"I promise you I will ask him at the earliest convenience," Margaret told him brightly. She did not

think it would take much to dissuade the marquis from including her cousin.

She was not wrong. When Thomas called that afternoon, she waited until her stepmother had exhausted her supply of superlatives in praising the upcoming visit before finding an excuse to send her from the room. Her stepmother went willingly enough, apparently content to overlook character flaws for a trip to the country.

"We must talk," she told him as soon as they were alone. "I need your help. Do you know my cousin, Reginald Pinstin?"

His face froze into a polite smile. "I believe we have met."

"You look none too pleased with that fact," Margaret surmised. "He wants to join us at Hillwater. Say no."

Thomas' smile became genuine. "No. That was easy."

Margaret returned his smile. "Quite easy. At least that's one subject on which we are agreed." Thinking how many others were less congenial, her smile faded. "What were you thinking to suggest this visit in the first place? My stepmother vexes you so I am surprised you don't cross your eyes when you visit. My father will run out of debate topics within a sennight. Your aunt will do nothing but bait me, and your sister will surely run screaming from the room within minutes of our arrival. Why would you possibly want to be alone with us for two months?"

He leaned back against the chair, at least as far as it was possible to do so in the withdrawing room. "I don't particularly wish to be alone with your father or stepmother. I do wish to be alone with you."

Warmth flared from her toes to her forehead. "Oh, I see."

He chuckled, reaching out to capture her hands. "Margaret, I have made my intentions clear. I'd like some time for the two of us to be together more often than is possible here in London. If we can survive two months in the country, with your family and mine under the same roof, don't you think that bodes well for our future?"

"Yes." She swallowed, unable to pull away. "Certainly. Oh, Thomas, are you sure about this plan? Has nothing I've done disturbed you to the point at which you question this courtship?"

"Not recently," he replied, and she knew he was hedging.

"Do not play with me," she demanded. "You said you wanted to court me, and I have gone along with you. But rides in the park and dinners with friends hardly constitute spending two months in each other's company."

"Do you have some terrible habit you have yet to confess?" he teased. "Do not tell me—you turn into a wolf by the light of the moon."

"Nothing so horrible." She sighed. "In fact, I do believe you have seen all my foibles."

"And I have not quailed," he replied, giving her hand an encouraging squeeze. "Besides the fact that our families will likely be at each other's throats within a few days, what else troubles you about this visit?"

She looked into his eyes and saw only concern. She ought to rejoice for an opportunity to spend time with him, to learn everything about him, even if it meant some secret. But the truth was, for once in her life, she was frightened, and she could not tell him what she feared. She who was so honest found it impossible to bare her soul and admit that the closer he got, the more she feared to lose him. It was far easier, and far safer, to love him from a distance than to risk the chance that he might turn from her altogether.

"Tell me the truth," she demanded, yanking back her hands. "If I submit to this visit, and if by some strange improbable act of God it goes well, will you offer for me? Would you want me as your bride?"

His smile deepened and he put his hands on her shoulders. She thought again that he meant to kiss her. Almost against her conscious will, her body leaned closer in anticipation. His gaze lingered on her mouth, and she could see a longing matching her own. Heart pounding alarmingly, she closed her eyes.

Thomas pulled her head to rest on his upper chest. She could hear the rhythm of his heart, just as fast and fierce as her own. "Margaret, I promise you. Unless something unforeseen happens, I fully intend to make you my bride."

"Oh." It was all she could seem to get out. Again she waited, knowing such declarations were normally followed by an impassioned kiss. His arms tightened around her; she could feel his strength. He rested his cheek against her hair. She could feel the tension in him. She pulled away.

"Thomas?" She frowned.

He rose. "I hope I have allayed your concerns, my dear. I am not trifling with your affections. Do we still ride in the morning?"

"Yes," she replied, deflated. He nodded in acknowledgment, bowed over her hand from a distance, and turned to go.

"Thomas," she said again and he paused, glancing back over his shoulder.

"Do you find me attractive?"

He started, then covered it with a laugh that could

only be called nervous. "My, but we are full of difficult questions today."

"I don't think of that as difficult," Margaret replied, struggling once again with her doubts. "It seems rather straightforward to me. One either finds someone attractive or one does not."

He ran his hand back through his hair, in an uncharacteristic move that mussed his normally carefully coiffured hair. "I'm not sure I'm up to more than one dire confession in a day."

Margaret wanted to pity him, but her heart was hurting too much. "In other words, you don't find me the least attractive. I don't think that bodes at all well for the future."

He stood for a moment more, then strode back to her, cupping her shoulders once again and glaring into her eyes. "Why can't you ever leave well enough alone?" he growled.

Margaret swallowed, heart once more pounding. "It's . . . it's in my nature, I think." In truth, she could not think at all with him standing so close. His chest was heaving as if he was making an extreme effort, his eyes tortured. As before, she thought surely he would kiss her, but again, he drew her into his embrace, letting her head rest against his shoulder.

"Can you hear that hammering?" he asked sharply. "That is my heart, demanding that I act like a savage beast and kiss you senseless. I am not going to do so. You ask whether I find you attractive? At this moment, I would cheerfully walk barefoot over burning coals to have you in my bed."

Margaret pulled away, staring up into his face for confirmation. He looked as frustrated as he sounded. She swallowed.

"I cannot grant you that, my lord," she managed. "I too believe some things should be saved for marriage. However, I do not think a kiss or two is out of the question.''

He let go of her and walked to the door again, clearly refusing to turn back this time. "Yes, it is," he replied. "I hope I have answered all your questions, Margaret. And if I haven't, I hope you'll have the kindness to ask me again some other time, preferably in a crowded room.''

Fifteen

Thomas sat on Nicodemus on the road above Hill-water Park, his estate on Coniston Water, and gazed out over the lake, wondering whether he might have gone insane. All his life he had set goals for himself, worked to achieve them, and basked in the glow of accomplishment. Sometimes he had worked harder than others. Intellectual pursuits came easy to him, as did riding, boxing, and most other sports. Standing his ground with Lady Agnes, debating in Parliament, and courting had been much harder. Courting Margaret Munroe was proving impossible.

He knew it had been propriety that had made him call on her the first time, pride that had started the friendship, and curiosity that had encouraged it. After his last meeting with her before coming north to prepare for the visit, however, he could no longer describe his interest with such mild language. The truth was that she stirred him as no woman had ever done. He did not understand it, but he could not deny it. Surely that alone was reason enough to suspect his sanity.

"I wouldn't mind having a try at that black," Court suggested as he rode up beside him on one of Thomas' other horses. "There was even a man's saddle in the tack that came with him, so surely she lets others ride him."

"Not necessarily," Thomas replied, thinking of what a bruising rider she was. It would not surprise him that she occasionally rode astride.

Court was not to be dissuaded. "Come on, DeGuis. What's the use of coming on ahead with such a beast if all he must do is fret in the stable?"

Thomas smiled, patting Nicodemus. "And he will fret. I've seldom met such a devoted horse. I swear he misses her." *As much as I do,* he amended silently.

"All the more reason for you to let me take him out for a run," Court insisted. "She need never know."

Thomas shook his head. "I have a feeling he'd tell her. Besides, I promised the lady I'd take good care of him. We went slowly getting here so as not to strain him. We should not press our luck now."

"Four days' ride from London didn't strain him," his friend replied with a snort. "I doubt two days in a full-scale gallop could strain him. But I surrender to your wisdom. I admit I would not want to be the one to tell Miss Munroe I had somehow damaged her prize animal." He cocked his head, eyeing Thomas thoughtfully. "You've settled on her, haven't you? This visit isn't just an excuse to get Catherine and me together. You're intending to offer for her."

Thomas sighed. "In truth, Court, I was beginning to think seriously on it. Now, I wonder at my own mind. We are so very different. Can two people find happiness from such different points of view?"

"Happiness?" Court replied with a chuckle. "And what novels have we been reading, old man? Some people have the luxury of marrying for love. You are marrying to continue the line. She's strong stock, I'll give her that. She ought to bear you strapping sons. What more do you ask for?"

Thomas frowned. "Is that all you want from Catherine? Somehow, I don't see my sister birthing strapping anythings. Is she less of a woman in your eyes because of that?"

Court had the good sense to look uncomfortable. "Certainly not. But Catherine is a DeGuis. She has years of breeding and connections to offer, which Miss Munroe does not. I was merely trying to point out her better qualities."

Thomas' frown deepened. "And her ability to bear children was all that came to mind? I would have added intelligence, a delightful sense of humor, and a heart worthy of her magnificent breast."

"I begin to think you are besotted," Court joked. "Marry her then, if you will. But do not let her Whiggish tendencies sway you. We need your votes solidly on the conservative side, DeGuis."

"If I didn't know better, I'd think that was a threat," Thomas growled. "I have never changed my vote to suit a friend, female or male." He looked at his ambitious friend pointedly.

"My word, you are touchy," Court muttered, urging his horse past Thomas to head down toward the little stone stables beside the house. "Perhaps you ought to have eaten more of Mrs. Tate's fish chowder we had for luncheon. The way you act, you'd think you were in love with the chit."

Thomas watched silently as the viscount rode away in high dudgeon, scattering the black-faced lambs that cropped the emerald lawn. In truth, he was not sure what to think. Love, the impassioned love the poets wrote of, had never seemed real to him. Certainly it must be more than a desire to hold a woman in one's arms. But was what he felt for Margaret love?

And, as Court had so ineloquently put it, did it matter? He hadn't loved Margaret when he had started this association he hadn't even considered he might fall in love. In actuality, love was only a messy side effect, one that threatened his well-made plans. If he loved Margaret, surely he'd be tempted to kiss her. And that he could not do, or he would lose her forever.

He gazed out over the azure waters of the lake. The deep color mirrored the cloudless sky above and framed the high fells beyond. Ravens darted among the beech and maple trees at the water's edge. A breeze stirred his hair and set Nicodemus to whickering over the unaccustomed scent of hay freshening. It was calm here, peaceful. Surely this was the place, as it had always been from his childhood, where he could focus on what was important.

As if in answer to his thoughts, his chest spasmed. Thomas caught his breath, jerking at the reins, and Nicodemus started. Fire raced from his gut to his throat and a giant hand gripped his upper chest, squeezing the air from his body, making it impossible to replace it. He struggled against the pain, even as he fought against the panic rising with it. Not again. The doctor had assured him the attack in December would not return. He was healthy, strong. There was no reason he should die as young as his father had. His heart could not simply give out.

As quickly as it had come, the attack dissipated. Thomas sucked in the summer air gratefully, collapsing over Nicodemus' mane to grip it with both hands. The Arabian shied nervously, turning in confused circles as Thomas took a deep shuddering breath. Forcing himself to straighten, he took up the slack in the reins and brought the dun back under control. His chest ached, his throat felt raw as if burned by some acid. He swallowed and felt as if he had eaten a brick. Had he wanted to focus on what was important? Here was his answer, just as Court had predicted. What he felt about Margaret was immaterial. What was important was to set up his nursery as quickly as possible, to ensure the continuity of the marquisette his family had managed for generations. That was his responsibility. And the most expedient way to do that was to offer for Margaret Munroe, as quickly as possible.

He had arranged for Court and himself to reach the estate a good few days ahead of the Munroes and his own family. Consequently, they were due at any time. Mr. and Mrs. Tate, the elderly couple who served as caretakers when he was not in residence, had already aired the small house, changed the bedlinens on all the four-poster beds, and been to Hilton two miles away for supplies. Of his many estates, Hillwater Park was by far the smallest. Its forced intimacy had been one of the reasons he had selected it for his time with Margaret. No country great house this—it was two stories with servants' quarters under the blue-gray slate roof, a square block center with a single wing extending off the southeast end nearest the lake. The walls were white-washed, the narrow windows darkly framed and shuttered. The Tates had planted red geraniums along the flagstone walk from the road to the stout oak door and down the path from the verandah overlooking the lake down to the shore. Behind the center block, the slope from the house to the shore was filled with roses, gladiolas, and daisies in wild abandon as if scattered by the hand of the master planter. Looking at it now as he rode carefully for the stables, he could think of no more fitting setting for his wild Margaret.

Regina Scott

Unfortunately, it was his own carriage that arrived first later that day, after he'd had only a little chance to rest from his attack. He handed his Aunt Agnes down, pausing to kiss her soft-skinned cheek as she leaned toward him.

"We passed the Munroe carriage outside Windermere," she told him. "They should not be far behind us. By the by," she continued as she moved toward the house, "Catherine moped all the way up here. If I didn't know better, I'd think she actually misses that Darton fellow."

Thomas' hopes rose. He had not had the courage to tell his sister that Court was coming along and had expected to have to endure her tears upon arrival. Now she glanced about as soon as she alighted and he did not think it was the view of the lake she sought.

"Might I hope you've noticed the gentleman awaiting you?" He smiled, nodding toward the lake where Court was tying a fly to his willow fishing rod.

Instead of brightening, she paled and stared at him, and his heart sank.

"Gentleman?" she gasped. "Thomas, who do you mean?"

Thomas sighed. "Viscount Darton, of course." He pointed to the tall silhouette against the bright waters of the lake.

Catherine shuddered. "Oh, Thomas! How could you invite him without consulting me?"

"I thought you needed time to know your mind," Thomas replied gently. "It is only two months. I promise you, if you are certain you will not suit by the end of that time, I will cry off for you."

She glanced toward the waters but her stare was unseeing.

"Catherine?" Thomas frowned.

She blinked, recollecting herself as if with difficulty. "I do not think you need to wait so long," she murmured. "I can tell you now that two months, two years, will not change my mind. I will not marry Viscount Darton."

She stiffened and walked with head high toward the house.

Thomas shook his head. His sister's determination did not bode well for the young viscount. But Court was nothing if not determined himself. If he decided Catherine was the woman for him, Thomas had no doubt Court would win her over.

A few minutes later, the Munroe coach pulled into the yard. He half-expected to find Margaret driving, but she was the first to alight, blue eyes merry. She favored him with a smile, then her gaze swept past him to the now-empty lake shore and across it to the quarry village at the foot of Coniston Old Man, the fell behind. Her eyes widened and she gazed back at him. "Oh, Thomas, it's beautiful!"

He smiled as well. "Yes, it is now."

She blushed, the color flushing up from the collar of her navy travel cloak to the roots of her marbled hair. Thomas had to fight the urge not to reach out and tuck some of the fly-away strands back into her topknot.

"Thank goodness, we're here at last," puffed Mrs. Munroe, clambering down from the carriage. "This is a lovely place, to be sure. Could someone please direct me to the main house?"

Thomas bowed to her, then waved toward the white-washed walls. "Hillwater is as you see it, Mrs. Munroe. I promise you the interior is grander than the exterior."

"I certainly hope not," Margaret remarked. "I find the exterior charming and much more comfortable than some grand house with more rooms than character."

Her stepmother looked doubtful, but her father, who had just alighted, was gazing thoughtfully at the lake.

"Trout?" he barked at Thomas.

"As big as your arm," Thomas promised with a grin.

Her father quirked a smile, rubbing his hands together gleefully. Thomas thought he might insist on trying immediately, but Mrs. Munroe cleared her throat and he hurried to follow her to the house.

"This is absolutely perfect," Margaret exclaimed beside him. "I cannot imagine a more lovely setting. Where have you put Aeolus?"

"In the stables, of course," Thomas replied, nodding to the stone building beyond the carriage. "And he is as eager to see you as I was."

Before he could think to stop her, Margaret darted around the back of the carriage, startling the grooms and the villagers hired to play footmen for the visit. Leaving them to deal with the baggage, he could only follow in her wake. He found her, one foot raised on the wood railing, nose-to-nose with the thoroughbred. Aeolus blew softly, nodding against her face, and if Thomas had not known better, he would have sworn the two were deep in conversation.

"And does he report satisfaction with his accommodations?" Thomas teased. "Or does he request the master bedchamber?" He reached out a hand and was pleased when the brute suffered his touch with only a roll of his eye.

"He is well satisfied," Margaret proclaimed, stepping down. "I knew you would take care of him, Thomas. But I had to say hello as soon as I arrived."

"I quite understand," he replied, tucking her hand in the crook of his elbow. "However, I'm not so sure what my aunt will think being upstaged by a horse."

"One creature is as good as another," Margaret quipped. His frown must have reminded her that he did not know the reference for she hurried to explain. "Your aunt once asked me whether I was the creature who had attracted your attentions."

Thomas sighed. "I'm sorry, Margaret. She had no right to be unkind. However, you have completely won her over. She and Catherine are eager to renew the acquaintance."

"Not nearly as eager as Aeolus, I'd wager," she remarked, but she did not pull away and Thomas succeeded at last in following her parents to the entryway. His chest still hurt from the morning's attack, and he felt as if he'd been holding his breath since the Munroes' arrival. He took a deep lungful of the clean lake air and felt himself relax. Everyone had arrived safely and appeared to be on relatively good behavior. Perhaps things would go smoothly for a change.

They entered the house and Margaret froze.

His aunt and sister had not gotten upstairs before the Munroes had entered. He had no idea what his aunt had said, but it had reduced Mrs. Munroe to a quivering pile of indignation and even Mr. Munroe appeared to have been struck dumb. Catherine was wringing her hands in dismay and appeared about to break into tears. But Margaret seemed oblivious to them. She was gazing across the entryway to where Court had just returned from the lake with his catch. He stood stiffly, eyes clouded and lips compressed as he met her stare. Her jaw was set and her blue eyes snapped fire. He had forgotten to tell her that Court would be joining them.

He had been right earlier. This visit was doomed. He had been insane to even suggest it. But then, he had already suspected as much.

Sixteen

"I do not know how I will last two months in that woman's company," Mrs. Munroe declared when they had been shown to their adjoining rooms. "Not even for you, Margaret. She is completely without sensibility."

"Now, now," Mr. Munroe muttered, patting his agitated wife heavily on the shoulder in an ineffectual attempt to calm her. "I was a little surprised by her remark but I'm sure she meant it in good taste."

"Oh, certainly, *you* take it as a compliment," Mrs. Munroe complained, jerking away from him to pace the warm plank flooring of the room Margaret had been given. Normally, Margaret was sure, her stepmother would have been enthusing about the simple elegance of the room with its carved wreathes of flowers bedecking the creamy white of the cornices, doorheads, and mantel. Now she scarcely noticed the decorations, or the fine Chippendale furnishings along the walls. Her antics might have been amusing, but Margaret still smarted that Thomas would spoil their time together by inviting an arrogant toad like Viscount Darton.

"What exactly did Lady Agnes say?" she asked, perching on the end of the mahogany four-poster bed and pushing a red-patterned cotton toile curtain out of her way.

"Only something about my noted intellect," Mr. Munroe supplied, going to stand by the white marble fireplace.

Mrs. Munroe glared at him before answering. "She said, and she was addressing your father, 'I heard you had a good head on your shoulders. Whatever possessed you to marry your wife?' "

Margaret choked and bit her lip to keep from laughing aloud. Her father looked away as if doing the same.

"Well," Margaret managed after a moment, "you should pity her, madame. That question sounds like something I'd ask."

"And if you'd asked it," her stepmother replied with a toss of her head, "you can be sure I'd box your ears. She is a terrible example of a society matron, Margaret. Do not be tempted to mimic her. I expect better behavior from you while we're here."

"You bait Lady Agnes," Margaret offered. "I'll bait Lord Darton."

"None of that now," her father put in with one of his rare moments of command. "Both of you will be on your best behavior. I won't have you spoiling what could prove to be a very pleasant holiday. Trout as big as your arm, he said."

"Oh, you and your fishing." Helen snorted in disgust and stalked toward her own room next door. "Wear the pink sarcenet tonight, Margaret. Even if we are in the country, I see no reason not to change for dinner."

"I will be sure to change," Margaret replied, going to close the connecting door before her stepmother could notice she had not agreed to change into the sarcenet. She set her back against the door and gazed about the room. It was bigger than the one she had at home and certainly more richly furnished. With twin windows facing the morning sun, she imagined it would be a cheery place to awaken. When the fire was glowing in the wood-framed marble fireplace, it would surely be a warm place in which to fall asleep. She could probably be very happy here if she did not have the firm suspicion that the happiness was to be short-lived.

It was even shorter than she had expected. After her father's command, she had thought at least her stepmother might be pleasant at dinner. She had certainly scolded herself into some degree of civility. While she still abhorred the pink sarcenet, she had been willing to don her green silk instead. With its square-cut neck and graceful skirt, it was as simply elegant as Hillwater. It whispered comfortingly to her as she followed her parents downstairs to the sitting room. The look of appreciation in Thomas' eyes when he bowed over her hand told her she had chosen well. Even Lord Darton thawed sufficiently to bow to her. Catherine looked sweet in a pink gown of watered silk, making Margaret thoroughly glad she had refused the sarcenet. Even Lady Agnes was more brightly gowned in rose. Neither Thomas nor the viscount had felt it necessary to wear the evening black of town, being dressed in navy and tan, respectively. All in all, it was a pleasant company who went in to dinner together.

The peace, unfortunately, did not survive the first course of the welcoming dinner. Mrs. Tate, who served as both housekeeper and cook, did not appear to be very talented in the kitchen. The roast was underdone and the Yorkshire pudding overdone and stiff. The trout that followed, however, melted in buttery warmth in Margaret's mouth.

"Now do you appreciate the merits of fishing?" her father demanded of her stepmother, who sat opposite him at the long oval table.

Mrs. Munroe gave a disparaging shrug but Lord Darton, seated at Thomas' left, brightened.

"Do you enjoy fishing as well, sir?" he asked.

"Delightful pastime," Mr. Munroe acknowledged between bites. "Practice every time we visit Wenwood."

"Ah, yes," Lady Agnes put in from Thomas' right, leaning around Margaret to address Mr. Munroe. "You have cousins there, I believe. Thomas is well-known to them."

Court coughed, and Catherine paled at the allusion to Thomas' first love, Allison. Thomas paused in his eating to scowl at his aunt. Margaret buried a laugh.

"I imagine he does," she replied cheerfully. "And I also imagine he had little time to fish while he was there. Frankly, I haven't had the opportunity to learn the sport. Perhaps I can rectify that while I'm here."

Thomas' scowl faded, and she thought he looked pleased at how she had turned the conversation back to more pleasant ground. She thought it rather adroit herself. But she could not congratulate herself for long, for Catherine opposite her was blinking as if confused and now the viscount was frowning.

"Surely you jest, Miss Munroe. I doubt fishing would be of any interest to a woman."

He had left himself so unguarded that she could not resist. "No more so than horse racing," she quipped.

Her stepmother choked, causing Catherine to jump in alarm. Mr. Munroe half rose from his seat as if to aid her, but she waved him down, reaching hastily for her glass. "Sorry," she murmured after a moment, red as all eyes remained on her with varying degrees of concern. "Must have been the fish."

Margaret gave it up and laughed. It was only a moment before she realized no one had joined her. Court actually looked shocked, as if she were making fun of her own stepmother. Shaking her head at their inability to see the humor in the comment, she attacked her own meat with gusto. Might as well be silent. Did not the Bible counsel to cast not one's pearls before swine? Glancing up, however, she met Thomas' gaze and saw the answering laughter in his eyes. Somehow the fish tasted heavenly again.

Unfortunately, they fared no better in the withdrawing room after dinner. Margaret was again struck by the simple beauty of the room with its west wall of windows overlooking the darkening lake. She longed to brush through the double glass doors to the verandah and garden beyond, but was forced to remain stiffly in the Queen Anne wing chair, smile pasted in place, while they waited for the gentlemen to finish their port. From the chair opposite hers, Lady Agnes' narrowed eyes watched Mrs. Munroe on the settee. Catherine's gaze darted nervously between them, as if waiting for another explosion. Mrs. Munroe's gaze seemed to be permanently fixed somewhere between the empty marble hearth and the Gainsborough landscape framed above it. Unlikely as it seemed, Margaret appeared to be the only one capable of saving the situation.

She rose, succeeding in drawing all eyes to her, and walked closer to the windows. "This certainly is a lovely house, Lady Agnes. Has it a history to match?"

Behind her, Lady Agnes sniffed. "Nothing of historical significance, if that's what you mean. My grandfather purchased it as a retreat for his new bride. She was a noted termagant."

Runs in the family, Margaret thought, but she gritted her teeth to keep the words inside.

"My brother, Thomas' father, was quite fond of the place as well," she continued when no one rose to the bait. "We spent part of nearly every summer here and often retreated here to celebrate family events like birthdays. And Thomas is want to spend the winter recess from Parliament here, though personally I do not see the charm of the place in the winter. It is entirely too desolate."

Remembering her feelings in the bedchamber, Margaret smiled. "There is a certain peace in an undisturbed vista. I can see why that might appeal to your nephew after the crowded halls of government."

"Perhaps," Lady Agnes allowed, "although I do not see why he keeps that woman as a cook. I must apologize for the dinner. It was inappropriately bad."

Margaret tightened her lips again to keep from asking what would be appropriately bad. Turning, she found Lady Agnes eyeing her with an unmistakable gleam of hope in her eyes. The woman *wanted* to start an argument. It struck Margaret that perhaps it was the only way she knew to make conversation. Another time she would have been pleased to oblige her, but Lady Catherine looked ready to faint and her stepmother appeared to be holding her breath in tension.

"Do you play whist, Lady Agnes?" Margaret tried, knowing her tone was overly bright.

Lady Agnes frowned. "Certainly. But I do not think it wise to start an entertainment until the gentlemen have arrived. I should speak to Thomas for keeping us waiting. It is most rude of him."

Margaret could not stand it. In her opinion, the only rude person in the house had just finished speaking. If she stayed in the room another minute, she would surely tell her so. The look of panic on her stepmother's face warned her that her intentions were apparent. Lady Agnes' eyes had brightened, and her mouth curved in a smile of victory. Catherine's eyes were huge and frightened.

"By all means," Margaret declared, striding for the door, "allow me to fetch him for you." It was the role of a servant, but she did not care. Anything to get away from the tension in the room. She was out the door and shutting it behind her before anyone could protest.

Ahead of her stretched the empty corridor with its cream-colored walls and dark plank flooring littered with colorful Oriental rugs. The dining room, she knew, lay around the corner and at the far end, next to the kitchen. Along the way lay a tantalizing number of doors, none of which anyone had seen fit to open when they had repaired here earlier. Her face lighting in a smile, Margaret set off to explore.

The first door opened on a library, the floor-to-ceiling inset bookcases filled with leather-bound volumes. She promised herself she would give them a serious study later in their visit, provided, of course, she survived that long. The room next to it surprised her, being cluttered with shelves and tables holding any number of amusements such as a polished set of nine-pins and a well-worn backgammon board. Dominating the space was a claw-footed billiard table. Sadly, none of the games appeared to have been used in some time, lying abandoned about the room with a patina of dust. She made herself another promise to see that the games were aired, though getting any of Thomas' guests except her father to play might be asking for a miracle.

Around the corner lay a music room, with a piano that was imposing large and polished for the simple

house. It gleamed in the light of the rising moon
outside. She wondered who played and scolded herself for hoping it was Thomas. Still, she could not see
the reticent Catherine having the fire to pound out
anything requiring feeling.

Now she was back to the sitting room and entryway,
across from which lay another set of beckoning doors
to the gardens. She marched resolutely past them
and paused before the dining room door. From inside came the companionable sound of male laughter. She grinned, pushing open the door.

"Well, at least the gentlemen seem to be enjoying
themselves," she declared.

The viscount's smile faded at the sight of her, but
Thomas' deepened. Her father chuckled.

"Couldn't wait any longer, could you? She was always that way as a child—walked early, sat her first
horse at eighteen months, started reading at two."

"Impressive," Court quipped with a wry smile. He
pushed back his chair and rose. "I suppose you have
come to fetch us."

"Just Lord DeGuis," she replied, wishing Darton
would take the hint and remain behind. "Lady Agnes
would like a word with him."

Thomas rose, frowning. "Is anything wrong?"

"Only if you think imminent murder troubling,"
Margaret answered. "Do come along and rescue your
sister, at least. I've been gone a good ten minutes and
I shall not vouch for what my stepmother and your
aunt are doing to each other."

Thomas came hastily down the room with Mr.
Munroe at his heels. Darton heaved a martyred sigh
and fell in behind.

"Is it truly that bad?" Thomas murmured to Margaret as they started down the corridor. He took her
arm.

"Worse," Margaret replied, relishing the feel of him against her. "Is there nothing your aunt enjoys more than arguing?"

"Nothing I have found," Thomas admitted.

"Well, we will have to keep looking or one of us will not survive the visit," she predicted.

Thomas squeezed her arm. "You were marvelous at dinner. If anyone can manage her, you can."

Margaret felt herself flushing. Why was it so little praise from this man warmed her so? She had not thought herself so desperate for compliments. "You give me too much credit, my lord," she murmured.

"On the contrary," Thomas replied, giving her an astonishingly warm look, "I'm beginning to think I haven't given you entirely enough."

On that warm note, they went in to battle.

Seventeen

By the time she went to sleep that night, Margaret knew she had found her challenge for the summer. Some people, most notably feather-brained peacocks like Lord Darton, might be bored by two months in the country. After the tense introductions and awkward welcoming dinner, she did not think boredom a fit description for her own emotions. But her own animosity at finding she had to endure a summer in Lord Darton's company quickly melted into sympathy. Thomas was clearly set to make this visit a success, flattering her stepmother, teasing his sister out of the doldrums, giving as good as he got from his delighted aunt, and cajoling Darton into a reluctant smile. She owed him no less of an effort. For his sake, she would attempt to be pleasant to Darton and to keep from rising to his aunt's bait too often. It was by far the most daunting job she had ever undertaken. But she had been known to enjoy a challenge, a trait she was quickly beginning to realize she shared with Thomas.

She rose at her usual time, changing quickly into her riding habit and dashing downstairs in hopes of finding a cup of tea before going to ride. She was surprised to find nearly everyone in the house in the dining room ready for breakfast. She raised her eyebrows at Thomas, who saluted her with his own tea cup as she came up the table to take an empty chair next to her father.

"Country house, country hours." He smiled, nodding to the footman to serve her. She selected a thick piece of bread and began to slather jelly on it from the ceramic bowl in front of her. Farther up the table, Lady Agnes smiled in greeting and Catherine nodded good morning. Lord Darton across from her managed a nod in place of a bow and quickly returned to his conversation with her father regarding the largest fish he had caught. His bragging, though languid, quickly bored her and she hurried through the bread in hopes of escaping to her horse before her stepmother could catch her. Mrs. Munroe, conspicuous for her absence, was sure to scold that she would come to the breakfast table in her riding gear.

"Would you like company this morning, Miss Munroe?" Thomas called from the top of the table. All conversation ceased, and every head turned in her direction. Margaret hastily swallowed her mouthful of bread to respond.

"Company, my lord?"

He waved toward her with his steaming cup. "You appear to be dressed to ride, an activity I believe you enjoy every morning at this time."

She smiled at him but before she could answer, Lord Darton cleared his throat. Heads swiveled in his direction.

"I believe," he said firmly, "that the gentlemen had agreed to go fishing."

Margaret's smile froze on her face even as Thomas frowned as if annoyed to be reminded. She would have liked nothing better than to tell the fellow to take his fishing rod to the far end of the lake and forget the way home. Still, she did not want to deprive

Thomas of the sport if he enjoyed it as much as her father did.

"I'll be riding every morning, as you noted," she replied to Thomas. "I'm sure you can join me another time if you have a commitment to Lord Darton this morning."

"And I'm equally sure Lord Darton will not miss me," Thomas said, eyeing Court as if he dared him to deny it. The viscount faced him for a moment, then turned his gaze to his plate with an ill-disguised frown. "Besides," Thomas added, "I believe Lord Darton had expressed an interest in a carriage ride about the area. Catherine, if you wouldn't mind obliging him?"

Catherine started, eyes darting between the young viscount, who looked willing, and her brother, who frowned at her sternly. It put Margaret in mind of a similar look she had seen often enough on her stepmother's face—it usually meant Margaret was supposed to do something for propriety's sake that she personally found disgusting. Did Thomas seek to occupy the viscount while he was busy with Margaret, or was there something brewing between Catherine and Darton? She liked Catherine enough to hope the latter was not true.

"I regret I cannot accompany Lord Darton this morning," Catherine said quietly, rising hurriedly. "Miss Munroe asked me to go riding with her, to show her the various paths about the estate. If you'll excuse me, I'd better change."

Darton rose hurriedly and bowed as she dashed past him. Standing, he eyed Thomas. "Then surely we should let the ladies enjoy themselves," he said, as if in challenge. "You will be free to join Mr. Munroe and me on the lake."

Thomas, ever the good host, managed a tight

smile. "Yes, so it appears." He turned to Margaret, deep blue eyes narrowed. "Another time, my dear?"

"Certainly," Margaret smiled graciously, wishing her stepmother had been present to see the polite facade she put on. She would much rather have had Thomas show her about, and she didn't much like having to agree to Catherine's lie about inviting her to ride. But she could sense fear and loathing from the girl regarding Darton and was not about to abandon her to the fellow's dubious charms. She finished her breakfast without having to do more than smile at other's witticisms, and went down to the stables to wait for Catherine.

The girl was a while in coming, and her puce velvet riding habit looked as if it had never been worn. Certainly it was cleaner, less crushed, and thicker than Margaret's, which was beginning to show its wear despite their maid's industrious attempts to refurbish it. The groom had saddled a small, dainty Arabian mare with a dappled coat, carefully helping Lady Catherine into the finely tooled side saddle. Margaret felt a little like a warrior maiden from some Norse myth riding Aeolus beside the girl.

Catherine rode stiffly and slowly, bouncing in the saddle despite the even gait of the Arabian. Aeolus was soon chomping on the bit and straining on the reins, ready to run. Margaret held him in check with difficulty—not from his strength but because she too longed to run along the stony tracks that led over the hillside above the house. Catherine, however, seemed content to plod along, pointing out the lake, the village beyond, and the towering mass of Coniston Old Man. Aeolus let out a snort of contempt and not long after, both Margaret and Catherine sighed in unison. The irony of it struck Margaret and she laughed out loud, the sound echoing off the slate hills around them.

Catherine hung her head. "I'm sorry, Miss Munroe. I shouldn't have said I'd come. Thank you for not calling me on the story. I know you do not like to lie."

"That I do not," Margaret confessed. "And for my reward, I'd like to know why I had to. What is it about Lord Darton that so disgusts you?"

"But I sensed you did not like him either," Catherine replied, rising her head in the first defiant act Margaret had seen.

"I cannot stand the fellow," Margaret agreed willingly. "He is an over-confident upstart with more ambition than sense. That does not signify. Why don't you like him?"

"Oh, I suppose he is a decent fellow, in his own way," Catherine conceded grudgingly. "Thomas seems to like him well enough."

"Why, I cannot imagine," Margaret intoned. "But that is beside the point. If you do not dislike him, why do you avoid him?"

Catherine picked at the saddle in front of her. "It . . . it is difficult to explain."

"You know I prefer the direct approach," Margaret encouraged her. "Say it straight out and we can have a good laugh or a good cry, if we must."

Catherine took a deep breath as if about to plunge into icy water. Margaret waited for some horrible story about the fellow having taken advantage of her.

"Have you ever been in love?"

Margaret grit her teeth to keep the smile in place. Aeolus sensed the tightening in her body and trotted forward. She reined him back beside Catherine.

"My, but people like to ask me that question," she replied.

Catherine colored. "I did not mean to pry. I meant in general, with any of your suitors."

"Of whom there are legion," Margaret teased, relaxing. "In love, eh? Well, yes actually."

"Oh, good," Catherine said with a sigh. "I'm so glad because Aunt Agnes never has, you see, and Thomas is a man and doesn't have the same feelings."

"So I've noticed," Margaret quipped.

Catherine did not seem to understand her attempt at a joke. "Just so. I simply must talk about it to someone or I shall swoon!"

Margaret eyed the woman riding next to her. "Don't tell me you're in love with Viscount Darton."

"No!" Catherine declared so ringingly that the mare shied. She guided her back to Aeolus' side with difficulty. "No, only please do not tell Thomas. I could never love Lord Darton. I'm already in love with someone else."

"Really?" Margaret asked, fascinated. "Who?"

Catherine turned to gaze at her, deep blue eyes drilling into Margaret with surprising intensity. Margaret stiffened her back.

"If I tell you, you must promise not to breathe a word of it."

"Let me guess," Margaret sighed. "Thomas knows nothing about the fellow, and if he did, he would disapprove."

Catherine nodded. "Most certainly. He is completely beneath me. Socially, that is," she hurriedly amended when Margaret scowled at the high-handed statement. "He is French, you see, and common born. But there does not live a more noble, gentle, sweet soul, I am convinced."

"And he is willing to marry you should your brother cut you off without a penny?" Margaret asked, suspicion rising. She had heard too many similar stories from the young ladies at Comfort House, only it was generally those girls who were deemed socially inferior.

Catherine sighed, tears pooling in her expressive eyes. "He has declared he cannot marry me at all. He is urging me to accept Lord Darton because the viscount can take care of me in the style to which I am accustomed. Oh, as if that mattered!"

"Then Viscount Darton has already offered for you?" Margaret asked with a frown, thinking of the fellow's rather boorish attentions.

"Not yet. I have been able to hold him off. But since Thomas arranged for us to be wed . . ."

"Thomas did *what?*" Margaret cried. Aeolus kicked up his heels and sprinted forward. This time she let him run a few moments before pulling him in and turning him back to Lady Catherine, who had reined in her own horse. An arranged marriage? How could he be so old-fashioned, so cold? Did he value love so lightly? Did he expect no feeling in his own marriage? Was that why he refused to kiss her? She forced the whirling questions aside and returned to Lady Catherine, schooling her face to impassivity.

"You didn't know?" Catherine asked.

Margaret shook her head.

"And it shocks you?"

Margaret could only nod.

Catherine sighed. "Thomas said it was only me who thought one should hold out for love. I'm glad to see I'm not the only one."

"No," Margaret replied sadly, "you're not."

"But it is still hopeless," she continued. "Thomas will never let me wed Christien!"

Margaret licked her lips, forcing herself to rise to

the challenge. "Just how big of a social gulf are we discussing? Is he a farmer? A laborer?"

"Heavens, no!" Catherine cried defensively. "He is an artist. He paints the most expressive pictures! I'll show you the one he did of Aunt Agnes. It's as if he illuminated her soul."

"So, he has a profession, if a chancy one," Margaret acknowledged. "And he obviously has your love. Are you sure you would be comfortable living in a set of rooms in London, say in someplace as unfashionable as Seven Dials?" She watched Catherine for any sign of concern over living in one of London's roughest districts, but the girl nodded with greater animation than Margaret had ever seen.

"Certainly," she insisted. "You have seen me, Miss Munroe. I do not delight in high society. Time to think, perhaps to read, would be most welcome."

"There'll be no servants," Margaret warned. "You'd have to cook and wash and clean on your own. And if you have a child, there'll be no governess or nanny to step in when you tire of playing."

"I would never tire of Christien's child!" Catherine cried. "I recognize I have much to learn, but I can do it, if it means being with Christien."

"Then," Margaret replied, "tell that to Thomas."

Catherine quailed, paling. "But I can't! He would never understand."

Margaret was beginning to think she was right, but her belief in truth was stronger. "You are going to face the censure of half the people in London," she told her sternly. "If you cannot tell a brother who loves you, how do you expect to hold your head up in public?"

"But he's so set on Lord Darton."

"He isn't marrying Lord Darton, you are," Margaret insisted. "The practice of arranging marriages is so old-fashioned as to be barbaric. The best thing you can do is to tell Thomas straight out, just as you did with me."

Catherine shook her head, tears falling. "Is there no other way?"

"None," Margaret replied sternly, though the girl's pitiful face was nearly her undoing. "Your brother is an honorable man, Lady Catherine. Even he would not expect you to marry where you do not love. Certainly, he would not do so."

"Then you are certain he loves you?" Catherine asked, choking back a sob. "He will understand my difficulties because he is in love as well?"

Margaret tightened her fist on the reins. "That I cannot promise. I do not know his mind. But if he answers you otherwise, please tell me. You see, I believe in the principle I am asking you to uphold. If Thomas does not, it is better I know now."

Eighteen

The visit was not going nearly as well as Thomas had hoped, and he was the first to admit that his hopes had not been overly high. He had thought managing his guests would be a challenge, but he quickly found that the only way to survive was to divide and conquer. Certain pairs were virtually impossible. Lady Agnes and Mrs. Munroe could not be in each other's company for more than five minutes before Mrs. Munroe was either livid or in tears. However, Court seemed to find Mrs. Munroe interesting. Thomas could not understand how they found conversational topics of mutual interest, but find them they did. And that was to the good, for Catherine still could not abide his company and spent her time with either her Aunt Agnes or Margaret, although she would settle for Mr. Munroe in a pinch. Lady Agnes plainly preferred a spirited debate with Mr. Munroe, but was happy to strike sparks off Margaret instead. By carefully coupling his guests, he was able to keep the peace, at least part of the time.

His own peace, however, remained elusive. First there was the matter of the attack. He had managed to slip away for a few hours to visit the physician in Hilton. Trained in the famed Edinburgh school, the fellow could have demanded a high price in London but had chosen the quiet Lake District for its beauty. Dr. Cranwell had interviewed him, asking him a number of questions about his activities, his sleeping patterns, and his meals. As was the wont of the learned gentleman from Edinburgh, he did not touch Thomas, but the swift delivery of questions was just as probing.

"Nothing you have said would make me believe your heart is weakening," the physician insisted. "Unfortunately, nothing you have said would lead me to another source of the attacks. Point to where you felt the pain."

Thomas pointed, feeling the fool bothering the man with what was surely some minor ailment. Cranwell's heavy brows drew together in a frown and he scribbled something on the paper he held before him.

"Have you heeded my advice?" he demanded. "Have you curtailed activities that might cause your heart rate to increase unduly?"

"I never thought of my life as boisterous," Thomas replied. "But yes, I've tried not to do anything out of the ordinary."

The physician consulted his paper again. "I hear you have been courting," he said to the parchment. "Is that going well?"

Thomas tried not to flush. "I do not see how courting signifies."

"Don't you?" Cranwell raised his gaze to study him and Thomas felt his cheeks heating. In fact, he felt exactly as he had when his father had caught him fingering the bridle of his prize hunter and dreaming of daring exploits. Neither dreaming of riding to the hounds nor dreaming of marrying Margaret was a heinous crime. He straightened his back and met the physician's gaze straight on.

Cranwell didn't fluster easily. "Scowl all you like, my lord. It is plain by your reaction that this courting is a matter of concern for you. The red in your face tells me your heartbeat has quickened just thinking about it. It is quite probable, my lord, that this is the matter that is causing these attacks."

"Ridiculous," Thomas replied with a shake of his head. "Surely modern medicine has progressed beyond the romantic notion that troubles in love result in a physical trouble of the heart."

"Do not discount the old stories," the physician said. "I've seen healthy young widows die within weeks of their husbands from no other cause than their hearts were breaking. I've seen other robust fellows keel over at their tables in a choleric fit because they had held in anger for too long. My advice to you, my lord, is to finish this courtship of yours as soon as possible. One way or the other, it could ruin your health."

Thomas had cause to remember the fellow's words in the days that followed, though he could not lend them much credence. There were plenty of other occurrences that made his heart beat faster—in annoyance—and he did not succumb to an attack. Court continued to try to charm Catherine, yet she avoided him whenever possible. Court, on the other hand, often used her absences to advantage, badgering Thomas about his support to the amendment.

"The Prime Minister fears to bring it to the floor," he confided when Thomas demanded to know why he was so fixated on the measure. "Liverpool is concerned that if we lose on such a key piece of legislation, Breckonridge might call for a vote of no confidence. This could open the door for the Whigs to seize power. We cannot let the liberals control the government."

"Certainly not," Thomas agreed. "But if the Prime Minister is so concerned, then he is right to hold up the amendment. Compromises can still be achieved that would make the bill more palatable to both sides."

"Compromises," Court sneered, and Thomas blinked at his vehemence. "Compromises will only weaken the measure."

"Or strengthen it," Thomas said quietly. "I think I understand your passion on this one, old fellow. It is your first bill. But there is no shame in compromising, if all win."

"An easy statement, DeGuis," his friend returned sharply though Thomas could see the viscount was considering his words. "Your political career is not at stake."

"Neither is yours if you will but see it," Thomas corrected him. "There will be other opportunities to make your mark."

"I haven't given up on this one yet," Court informed him before striding from the room.

Much as the viscount's determination concerned him, however, Thomas had another matter far more troubling to deal with. Since the morning of the day after his guests had arrived, Margaret had distanced herself from him. He had feared the intimacy of the estate would force his hand, but she did not push him. Indeed, in the first week they had been there, she had spent more time with Catherine than she had with him. He supposed he should count it a blessing—without being alone with her, he was not put in the position of kissing her. That would certainly have increased his heart beat. However, he missed their moments together. And he wondered whether he had done something to offend her. Accordingly, the morning of the second week of their visit, he determined to rise with the sun in hopes of catching her before she started on her morning ride. Unfortunately, the day proved cloudy and he jerked awake barely ten minutes before eight. Thrusting his protesting valet aside, he hurriedly donned shirt, trousers, and boots, and, grabbing his cravat in one hand, dashed down to the stables.

One glance about the wood-framed stalls told him he was too late. Aeolus was nowhere in sight. He threw the cravat onto the straw in frustration. Trust Margaret to do something out of character, just when he was trying to make amends. He turned to start back to the house when there came the sound of pounding hooves. He melted into the shadows as Margaret rode through the doors of the stable.

She patted the horse as he slowed, head bobbing and snorting, obviously ready to keep running. Thomas stepped from the shadows, but before he could speak, she slid from the saddle.

"I don't suppose you'd care to join Nicodemus and me in a ride?" he asked. Then he started as she turned to stare at him.

He was sure his eyes must have been just as wide. Gone was the worn blue velvet riding habit he had seen so often. In its place were a pair of men's leather breeches, molded to her frame; a lawn shirt, buttoned over her magnificent chest; and a pair of Hessian boots well dusted from use. Her hair was braided down her back, silver running like ribbon through the black. The gentleman's saddle, which Court had commented upon, lay firmly in place across Aeolus' broad back. She had clearly gone out early so no one would see her.

But as she continued to stare at him, he realized he looked no less disheveled. Without the cravat, his own lawn shirt was open at the neck and hastily crammed into buckskin breeches. He hadn't even troubled to comb his hair, and his cheek must be shadowed with a morning's growth of beard. His unkempt state did not seem to trouble her. In fact, if the blush creeping over her cheeks was any indication, she was as fascinated by his appearance as he was with hers.

She shook herself awake with obvious difficulty. "Good . . . good morning, my lord," she stammered.

"My lord?" he asked, stepping closer. The gelding shook his head in warning and flattened his ears. Thomas halted. "I thought we had graduated to Thomas."

"No," she replied, licking her lips. "This morning we are definitely back to my lord."

He wasn't sure whether that was a compliment, or a complaint. He decided to follow her usual forthright lead. "Have I done something to offend you?"

"No, nothing," she said hurriedly. Had she been anyone else, he would have thought she was dissembling. With Margaret, he could only take her at her word. She obviously sensed his confusion, for she hurried on. "It's simply that I'm not used to seeing you, that is, I've only dreamed, that is, you look so . . ." she trailed off lamely, patting her horse and avoiding his gaze. She cleared her throat. "Aeolus and I would be delighted to join you, Thomas."

Grinning, he hurried to saddle the Arabian. A groom poked a sleepy head from the overhead loft, and, seeing Thomas, scurried down to help. Within minutes, he had the dun ready. Margaret turned the thoroughbred and Thomas followed her out of the stable into the morning light. The groom hurried forward to help her to remount. Thomas wondered how she had managed to get on the brute of a horse alone, but he did not intend to let her do so again. He elbowed the groom aside.

"Allow me," he murmured, placing his hand on either side of her slender waist. She stiffened, eyes widening once more. Her own hands clung to his as if she would push him away. He stood next to her for a moment, blue eyes locked onto blue. He could see his own reflection in the depths of hers. He could also see her throat move as she swallowed nervously. The insane notion of kissing that graceful neck begged acknowledgment. More, it demanded action. He heaved her up into the saddle. Letting go of him with hands that visibly trembled, she slung one leg over the saddle to ride astride and kept her face resolutely forward as he went to mount Nicodemus.

She followed him, rather docilely for Margaret Munroe astride a powerful black thoroughbred, up the slope to the track that ran along the lake. After a few moments, she brought the black alongside the dun. The Arabian had grown used to riding with Aeolus; his step did not falter. Aeolus mouthed the bit as if to protest being held to so sedate a canter, then settled into a begrudging walk.

"They seem to have accepted each other," Thomas remarked.

"Or at least agreed to a truce," Margaret answered with a chuckle.

"Would that our families were so easy to sway," Thomas replied.

"Perhaps they will be, with time," she allowed. She glanced out over the waters of the lake, sparkling in the early morning sunlight. "Catherine tells me you arranged her marriage."

Thomas frowned, wondering about the sudden change of subject. "Does that trouble you?"

"Greatly," she admitted. "Marriage is too important to leave the choice to someone else."

"I agree that marriage is an important step," Thomas replied, unwilling to argue with her when he was just getting back on better footing. "So important, in fact, that it should be decided by wiser minds than that of a twenty-year-old woman."

"I'm just one and twenty," she countered. "Do you find me incapable of determining my own husband?"

Thomas smiled. "Certainly not. But you are not Catherine. Do you find her capable of determining a suitable husband?"

She was surprisingly quiet for a few moments. Then she sighed. "In truth, I don't know. Sometimes she strikes me as an excessively silly widgeon, entirely too wrapped up in herself."

Although part of him agreed with her, he could not help but defend his sister. "Catherine was gently reared, Margaret. You must not judge her against your standards."

"Gently reared? By Lady Agnes?" She was plainly skeptical, and he found himself wondering indeed how different his sister's life had been from Margaret's. Certainly, they had had the privileges of wealth, as well as the noted DeGuis composure. But did that mean that Catherine should be allowed to be any less honest or forthcoming?

"Perhaps I haven't been the most attentive of brothers," he admitted with a sigh. "Perhaps I should have worked harder to draw her out. But she is as she is. And I still stand by the fact that she is ill-equipped to make so important a decision."

"But it is her life, Thomas," Margaret protested. "It seems to me she is entitled to make her own mistakes."

"And being the wiser older brother, I cannot shield her from some of them?" he pressed.

Margaret eyed him, somewhat cynically he thought. "And just how wise are you about marriage, Thomas? You haven't exactly managed to get yourself a bride."

He wanted to bridle up, demand an apology, but she was looking at him so intently that he could not deny her words. He gazed out over the lake instead. "You cut right to the heart, as usual. No, I haven't been married. But I love her and I want to make sure she is well-settled. No one is forcing her to wed Darton. If she has someone else in mind, she has only to say so."

"There, I knew you'd be sensible!" she declared, and he turned back to find her beaming at him. "You should tell Catherine that. She needs to hear it."

"I have told her so. Repeatedly. Why is it no one listens to me?"

Margaret laughed.

Thomas could not help but sigh. "Oh, how I've missed that sound."

She immediately sobered, reddening. "Do not tease me, my lord. Despite your previous compliments, my stepmother insists that my laugh is my least endearing trait."

"Stepmothers," he informed her, "are occasionally wrong." Her blush deepened, but she did not brighten. He frowned, wondering how to bring back the smile to her face. He had had entirely enough of serious topics for the morning. He pulled the dun up short, and Margaret reined in Aeolus. Thomas pointed to an outcropping of rock about a quarter mile distant. "See that slate slab overhanging the trail? First one there gets to name the prize."

"You're on!" she cried. He did not see her signal the black, but Aeolus sprinted into a gallop even as he touched his heel to Nicodemus' flank. They tore down the track, horses' hooves churning the pebbles underfoot. Trees flashed past. Birds shot out of thickets in surprise. A rabbit bolted off the track to ricochet down the slope beyond. Ahead of him, Margaret flattened herself over the saddle, plainly urging the black to fly. Her braid flung out behind her like a flag. Thomas bent low as well, murmuring to Nicodemus over the sound of the hooves. The dun stretched, but he could not catch the black. Margaret shot past the outcropping a good head in front of him.

They slowed the horses, pulling them back into a canter, then a walk and finally stopping on a wide spot in the track over the side of the lake. Margaret's chest was heaving as hard as her horse's.

"You won," he acknowledged.

She laughed, and he felt his arms pimple in goose flesh. "Yes, I won. You sound surprised. Do you still forget that I can ride? Come now, sir. It was you who called the race and set the stakes. Help me down so I can claim my prize."

He jumped easily from the saddle, heartbeat quickening more than when he had been racing. Dr. Cranwell would scold if he knew, but Thomas found he did not care. Striding to her side, he held out his arms and she slid obligingly into them. As he set her onto the ground, the light of laughter in her eyes was replaced by a stronger emotion. He felt it as well, building inside him. But he could not seem to let go of her.

"I claim," she murmured, watching him, "a kiss."

More than anything he wanted to grant her request. But it would spoil everything he had worked to achieve. He released her and stepped back. "No. Out of the question. I thought we'd settled that."

She frowned in obvious vexation. "I'm sure it's against some social code to insist, but you leave me no choice. Will you break your promise? You said the winner may set the prize."

"I assumed I would be the winner," Thomas quipped without thinking. Her frown only deepened.

"I do not believe you are so arrogant," she declared. "Even if you were, now that I have bested you beyond expectations, you refuse to honor your word? What kind of gentleman is that?"

He could not look at her. The hurt in her eyes he was sure was mirrored in his own. "Ask anything else, Margaret," he murmured, watching the lake. "Not that."

She was silent for a moment then sighed heavily. "Thomas, you exasperate me beyond measure. However, if you insist, I will pick another prize." She waited expectantly. She was giving him another chance to kiss her, or at least to explain why he refused. He could do neither. Even caring for her as he did, his heart wasn't ready.

"I'm afraid I must insist," he replied with forced coolness.

"Very well." She sighed again. "I suppose you could teach me to fish after breakfast. You and my father seem to find it fascinating. Perhaps it would be diverting."

Her tone was so begrudging that he had to chuckle. "Very well, then, fishing it shall be. Just as you wish."

"Not in the least," she replied, leading Aeolus to

a boulder, where she hurriedly mounted before he could so much as reach out a hand to touch her. "If I had my wish, I would have no further doubts as to your feelings." She turned the horse and rode ahead of him.

Thomas sighed, climbing back into Nicodemus' saddle. "That's what I'm afraid of," he muttered to himself.

Nineteen

If Thomas had been concerned that Margaret was too quiet before their ride, he immediately realized it had been a blessing. From then on, she seemed determined to discover the reason he refused to kiss her. She tried asking him in her forthright manner, but he managed to turn the topic aside with a joke, steering her toward his Aunt Agnes and effectively stopping that line of conversation. Even Margaret knew there were some things one did not discuss in front of his termagant aunt. Undeterred, she pressed the question the next time they were alone. He ended up walking out of the conversation, only to have to apologize later for his rudeness. Since then, she had been more careful in her attempts to broach the subject. Unfortunately, he was no more comfortable answering her.

He knew he could not avoid her forever. She was full of passion, and her feelings in all aspects sought physical release. When she danced, he could see the joy in her graceful movements. When she rode, she was one with the horse. When she gave of her time, she gave of herself. When she laughed, she laughed with all her heart, and most of her body. Why should she love any differently?

Her comment after their last race troubled him the

most. She had said she could not be sure of his feelings. Small wonder, for he could not be sure of them himself. He enjoyed her company, more so than anyone he had ever met. She had a refreshing way of looking at the world that invariably raised his spirits. He desired her, that was beyond question. And certainly he cared about her to the point that he wanted to see her happy.

So, how could he tell her the man who was courting her was not willing to be physical about his growing emotions? Even if he could let go of his fear of rejection, there was the matter of his kiss. How could he explain that? "My dear Margaret, I shall in all ways be an exemplary husband, but for one small matter. My kisses are no more than instructive, should one wish to be instructed on how *not* to kiss." Or perhaps, "I have been told my ability to kiss is less than most men. I hope you don't mind." He could of course follow her lead and simply demonstrate the matter by kissing her, but the thought of seeing her anticipation melt into dismay or worse, disdain, was too painful to bear. He would simply have to be strong and stick to his original plan, Dr. Cranwell's advice not withstanding. Only when he and Margaret were wed and he knew she could not reject him would he attempt physical intimacy.

Unfortunately, he found his own willpower a formidable enemy. They were thrown together constantly. This intimacy had also been part of his plan, but that fact did not comfort him. Instead of growing closer, as he had hoped, they were becoming more tense with each other. Margaret seemed to feel that the only way he could prove he cared for her was to kiss her. Yet that was the one thing he could not do.

They rode together every morning now. Most mornings they raced, although Thomas was careful not to repeat his mistake and suggest an ambiguous prize. She was a worthy opponent; in fact, he was never again sure of the outcome of their races. She won as many times as he did. Either way, she was always glowing with pleasure when they finished, and it took every ounce of his will not to pull her into his arms.

While their guests fished or read or strolled about the area, they usually spent the mornings wandering about the estate or driving to one of the nearby villages. Sometimes one or both of her parents joined them. Mr. Munroe seemed to be enjoying the visit, being one of the few who could engage Lady Agnes in conversation for any length of time. He also spent considerable time on the lake, bringing home trout that Mrs. Tate delighted in preparing for him until Mrs. Munroe declared she never wanted to see another helping of the tender white fish. She was still having a difficult time with his family, being the favorite victim of his aunt's cutting tongue. The one thing they had found that she could enjoy was the garden behind the house.

Both Margaret and her stepmother delighted in the riot of blooms. He had not realized the roses were declining until Mrs. Munroe cornered him one day. In one of the few times she had ever confronted him, she told him in no uncertain terms that his gardener was neglecting them.

"Really," Thomas commented, eyeing the lush green bushes beyond the verandah. The path between them was so overgrown one could scarcely walk through. "They appear to be healthy to me."

"Healthy they may be," she replied with a sniff, "but they have not been pruned, nor have the dead blossoms been cut off, for ages. You will not get many more flowers at this rate, my lord. Something must be done."

Knowing how busy his visitors were keeping his meager staff already, Thomas did not have the heart to add to their duties. Here again, Margaret came to his rescue. She and her stepmother had volunteered to take over the care of the gardens. Now, while he could not in truth say they looked any less wild, one could at least wander through them to appreciate the jungle.

He found himself marveling in more than one way at Margaret. People he did not know called and waved to her now when they passed. A farmer was pleased to present the last born of his black-faced sheep for her delighted cuddling. Jim, the son he never knew his caretakers had, handed her a string of trout, still dripping and wiggling, only to be met with praise and laughter, for she had yet to catch a fish, much to her chagrin. From Margaret he learned that the caretaker's cottage needed repairs (they had been too awed of him to ask) and the local church could not afford hymnals (a fact he quickly agreed to rectify). Most of all, her attentions to his aunt and sister made him realize that he had been neglecting them as much as the roses.

Before coming to the lake, he had often found the company of his aunt or sister difficult. Now it did not appear any more easy for Margaret, yet she did not seem to try to avoid them. In fact, she encouraged them to reach beyond themselves. She convinced Lady Agnes that her strident voice was perfect for declaiming, and lately he had had the singular pleasure of listening to the woman read from the works of Shakespeare. Her sharp mind and projecting tones were indeed theatrical, and all his guests declared that she was a success. Margaret was also the one to drag Catherine into the little used game room for a round of nine pins. To his surprise, he found his sister was a whiz at swinging the little wooden ball about in just such a way as to constantly strike all nine of the pins from their polished wood base. Even Court had been unable to beat her, and Thomas had been treated to the sight of Catherine actually smiling in the man's presence.

That smile was one of the few Catherine had bestowed on anyone. She had always preferred solitary amusements, but he had hoped company, especially Court's company, would be able to draw her out. Instead, she was wont to disappear for more than an hour each day. Once he found her down by the lake and another time near the gate to the estate. Both times she had confessed the need to escape the attentions of their guests. He took that to mean Court. He had clearly picked the wrong man for her. It was another sign that he had not taken the time to know his sister well enough to understand what she might look for in a mate.

He admitted as much to Court one night after the ladies had retired to the garden to hear Mr. Munroe expound on the constellations that glittered over the lake.

"Don't see how you can say that, old fellow," Court protested, stretching out long legs to prop his feet on the stone railing of the verandah. "You've been almost a father to Lady Catherine, and I daresay Lady Agnes would not have a home but for you." He accepted the port the footman offered. Thomas waved his aside.

"My aunt has a patrimony from our grandfather," Thomas corrected him, listening to the murmur of Mr. Munroe's voice beyond the trellis of roses. Margaret's flowers perfumed the night and he inhaled deeply. "She has only stayed with us all these years for Catherine's sake. She told me once she longed to travel but was waiting for us to get settled. I know she is godmother to several other people with whom she corresponds, although she seldom gets to visit, thanks to our neediness. Watching her enjoy Margaret's company, I realized I have taken her very much for granted. Small wonder the woman rails to get attention."

"She rails even when you give her attention," Court commented. "It is in her nature, I think. Thank goodness, your sister did not inherit the trait. Although I would not be surprised if you are about to marry another of the same ilk."

Thomas raised an eyebrow. "Do you still find Miss Munroe so objectionable? I thought a few weeks in her company would change your mind."

"Sorry," Court replied, taking a careful sip of the port. "She simply isn't my type. I'm somewhat surprised she is yours. But you seem rather contented in her company."

"Contented?" Thomas barked out a laugh. "Contented is hardly the word."

The viscount frowned. "Then you are masking your true feelings? Are you having second thoughts about this courtship?"

The conversation was too close to the truth for Thomas' taste. He turned the topic aside. "No more so than you are. I have not seen you much in my sister's company. Have you decided not to pursue her then?"

"One cannot pursue someone who does not wish to be chased," Court replied with a sigh. "Your sister is lovely, unobtrusive, and softly spoken. I think she would make an ideal wife. Only she does not agree that I should be the husband.

I hate to cry off, DeGuis, but I'm not sure this deal was well considered."

Now it was Thomas' turn to sigh, thinking of Margaret's assessment that his sister was entirely too wrapped around herself. He still felt she needed someone like Court to draw her out. "Perhaps you are right. But I'd like you to give it one more try. Her birthday is in two weeks. With any luck, we can make it special."

Court's eyes lighted. "A birthday? That might be just the ticket to spark some interest. Although I'm not sure what would amuse your sister."

"Not only my sister," Thomas replied, "my aunt as well. Lady Agnes and Catherine share the same birthday."

"It couldn't be easy," Court remarked with a sigh. "Ah, well, it will be a quiet affair at any rate. There's not many to invite this far from civilization."

"Oh, I don't know," Thomas mused. "I saw that Lord Rothbottom and his clan had arrived for the summer. They were in church last Sunday. You may have noticed them: tall fellow with the slender wife and four daughters."

Court eyed him. "All of whom were staring at you and me. I swear the oldest was salivating. Is there no one else?"

"The vicar and his wife? And it's possible the Byerslys have rented Hillcastle for September. They did a couple of years ago. They usually bring one or two people for company. Their oldest son would be five years your junior."

Court shook his head. "Worse and worse! Still, I suppose he might be of interest to the Rothbottom daughters. Take them off our scent. But what could you do with such a motley collection?"

What could he do indeed? He was having a difficult

time as it was keeping his assorted guests entertained and polite. Add four girls fresh from the schoolroom, their matchmaking parents, a young man ready to sow his wild oats and his parents who were determined to keep him from doing so, and the overly fastidious vicar and his equally stuffy wife. They would never find anything in common. Thomas closed his eyes.

"I don't suppose," Court suggested quietly, "that we might pawn the whole affair off on Miss Munroe? I imagine it would entertain her to no end. And we might get in some uninterrupted fishing."

Thomas opened his eyes, smile spreading. It was an impossible challenge that would delight an elderly woman and a shy young lady, not to mention brighten the otherwise quiet summer for most of the gentry in the area. It would take imagination, flare, and good humor. Margaret would adore it.

She was as enthusiastic as he had hoped when he broached the subject the next morning.

"A double birthday party!" she cried, clapping her hands. "Of course, we must make the day special. We certainly don't want to be as ostentatious as the prince who has the whole of the navy do maneuvers and lights up the skies over Brighton, but we shall contrive. Do they allow fireworks over the lake?"

Thomas cringed. "Perhaps something more quiet for our natural surroundings?" he suggested tactfully.

To his relief, she nodded. "Yes, you are right. Catherine wouldn't want anything too loud or overly bright. She would want something classical, perhaps."

"Just so," Thomas murmured, letting out his breath. "I believe there is a chamber group at Windermere."

Margaret frowned. "That would be good. Do you know anyone who would be willing to wear fish tails?"

Thomas choked back a laugh. "Fish tails?"

"Well, with this lake, one would think we could have mermaids," Margaret countered, still frowning. "Although now that I think of it, perhaps the Lady of the Lake would do better. Something chivalrous, courtly."

Thomas patted her shoulder. "I have faith you will think of something suitable."

She laughed, and he smiled at the sound. "It may be perfectly suitable in my mind, Thomas, but I could never be sure you or Hillwater would be ready for it. If I promise to explain the plan to you before I put it into action, would that ease your mind?"

He grinned. "Immensely. And if I know you, you will expect dancing."

Her eyes twinkled. "But of course! What use would a chamber group be if not to play for us to dance?"

"What indeed?" Thomas took her hand and kissed it. He had intended the gesture as appreciation for her generous willingness to help, but the feeling of her flesh beneath his lips did strange things to the rest of his body. His gaze traveled up the sleeve of her gown to her graceful neck, her determined chin, and those luscious lips. She was staring at him again. He dropped her hand and cleared his throat. "I look forward to hearing your plan, Margaret." With steps that were not as steady as he would have liked, he quit the room.

He had prided himself on his reserve, he thought as he walked down to the lake. That was the hallmark of the DeGuis family—calm, composed, solid as a rock even when storms surrounded. Being around Margaret these last few weeks had made him realize that he was using that reserve as an excuse to distance himself from those around him. In some circumstances, he supposed, it was warranted. There were always those who sought to flatter him into doing their bidding in Parliament, those who thought getting closer to him would benefit their careers, their fortunes, or their status. It was easy to turn a cold eye or a blank face to their attempts. It was inappropriate for him to do so with his family and friends.

Moreover, it was inappropriate of him not to put his love into action. Margaret had praised his support in Parliament of certain bills that would help people in their everyday lives. At the moment, he did not feel that his scholarly debates had been very useful. Margaret volunteered her time, working directly with those in need, even those everyone else chose to pretend did not exist. He had been shocked then; it made perfect sense now.

No, in his attempts to distance himself from his heartache he had hidden his heart away from anyone who might have needed it. Dr. Cranwell's advice had merely been another excuse. The good physician was wrong. Thomas was wrong. He would never fully appreciate Margaret's living in the moment if he was not willing to open himself to others. He resolved to work on the trait.

He started in little ways, like listening for the concern behind his aunt's scolds and thanking her when the advice was sound. He had a spirited debate on the merits of the Poor Laws amendment with Court, giving the young viscount additional food for thought. He took Mr. Munroe fishing and laughed at his stories of Margaret growing up. He complimented Mrs. Munroe on the work she had done in the garden and asked her advice on how to expand it. He took Catherine riding and confessed he knew little about marriage, even if it was his duty to arrange hers. She did not seem to appreciate the sentiment, but he thought her tension eased some.

As the days passed before the party, he found himself enjoying his visitors more and more. Catherine smiled and actually teased him at breakfast one morning. Lady Agnes' scolds seemed to have lost their teeth. Court asked his advice in rephrasing the bill. Even Mrs. Munroe could unbend in his company, taking him aside one day to make him promise he would be good to her Margaret. He thought at first some strange miracle had taken place that they were all behaving better. Then he realized the miracle was his own change of attitude. And that change was entirely due to Margaret.

He had never thought she fit the picture of his marchioness, but he was ready to concede that she was more than he had ever hoped for. He could envision a rather pleasant life together, once she got over her disappointment of his kiss, of course.

He would propose the night of the party.

Twenty

Margaret hadn't enjoyed herself so much in a long time. She had thought two months in the country might prevent her from doing any good deeds. Certainly she would miss her visits to Comfort House. But she had always wanted to plan a party. Her stepmother had never allowed her to so much as come near the planning process on the few dinner parties they had given, reminding Margaret of her noted eccentric tastes. In the case of planning a party for Catherine and Lady Agnes, however, Margaret's tastes had nothing to do with it. She was planning a party for their enjoyment, and she threw herself into the process as much as she did any of her activities.

It was certainly a challenge. Almost immediately she gave up the notion of doing anything that would surprise them. Clearly this was something she had to do with their full cooperation.

Lady Agnes, of course, had definite opinions.

"Dozens of people," she maintained. "That is the secret to a good party—dozens of people with whom to converse."

Knowing the lady's penchant for alienating everyone she spoke with, Margaret could well imagine it took several dozen people to fill an evening. "Your nephew has invited a number of people who are visiting the area for the summer." She consulted the list Thomas had made her. "The Rothbottoms, Byerslys and their guest, and of course the vicar and his wife."

Lady Agnes sighed. "Very well. I suppose that is the best we can do in the wilderness."

Catherine, on the other hand, was less demanding.

"A quiet evening," she told Margaret as they strolled through the gardens. "Cards, perhaps, or maybe Aunt Agnes would consent to read again."

"What about dancing?" Margaret put in.

Catherine paused to bring a blossom to her nose. She considered it carefully for a few moments before responding. "I suppose dancing would be acceptable. I have heard it is one of your favorite pastimes."

Margaret felt herself blushing as red as the rose in Catherine's hand. "In truth it is. But I don't want to influence you with my tastes. This party is for you."

Catherine smiled at the rose. "But you have influenced me, Miss Munroe. I find myself growing bolder just watching you."

"Have you told Thomas about Christien, then?" Margaret prompted hopefully.

"No," Catherine answered with a sigh. "Thomas has changed. I feel it. But he is still set on arranging my marriage. I am simply not convinced he will release me from this agreement with Lord Darton. But I assure you, I will never marry him." The petals of the rose fell between her fingers, crushed by her grip. Margaret grabbed her arm and pulled it away.

"Lady Catherine, you must do something!" she cried, shivering at the intensity of the woman's gaze. "It is unnatural to keep this amount of emotion bottled up inside."

Catherine laughed, but the sound held no joy. "I'm a DeGuis. We keep everything inside." Margaret released her and she offered a smile, though it held little warmth. "And speaking of keeping everything inside, how does my brother fare? I keep expecting him to announce your engagement."

Now it was Margaret's turn to look away. "We have reached no agreement," she told her. "You are correct that he keeps his feelings close."

"Perhaps the party will bring them out," Catherine mused, resuming their walk. "Your father told me that he had given Thomas permission to marry you when he could waltz. If we have dancing at the party, you may get your proposal."

"I doubt he has had the opportunity to learn," Margaret replied, still troubled by the woman's attitude. Could Thomas' reticence to kiss her be simply this deep reserve, or did he too keep secrets bottled up inside? She did not like to think what happened to an overfilled bottle. At best, it spilled; at worst, it exploded. "Besides, have we not agreed that you do not find dancing amusing?"

Catherine eyed her and quickly looked away. "If you can get my brother on the dance floor, I promise you it will amuse me no end. By all means, let us have dancing."

Margaret wished she felt better about the comment. Something else seemed to be driving Lady Catherine than the interest of seeing her brother waltz. Crafting an event that would please both her and her aunt would clearly take all Margaret's enthusiasm, intelligence, and creativity. It also forced her even more frequently into Thomas' company, as she asked him questions about his family, their customs, and their entertainments.

From him she learned that the game room had seen little use in their lifetime. His own father's health had prevented him from enjoying it.

"He was ill all his life, then?" Margaret asked, surprised.

Thomas nodded, fingering a toy soldier who had escaped the larger drum of them on the table nearby. "I think it was a foregone conclusion most of his life that each day was an unexpected blessing. I do not seem to be able to share that attitude."

"But you're strong and healthy," Margaret protested. "You seem to have broken the trait of dying young."

To her further surprise, he paled. "We none of us know when our time will be up, Margaret."

She linked her arm in his and gave the firm muscle a squeeze. "All the more reason to enjoy the moment, Thomas."

He patted her hand on his arm, granting her a wry smile. "Yes, I can safely say you've tried to teach me that lesson."

Now it was her turn to pause. "Not well enough," she muttered, releasing him. "If I had, you'd have kissed me long since."

"Let us not quarrel," he replied over-brightly, going on to point out activities Catherine had enjoyed as a child. Margaret didn't listen at first, wanting only to give him a good shaking. Did he not know the wall he put between them? Worse, did he know and not care? What was it about her that kept him from giving her his heart?

She had worried that there would be many things on which she and Thomas would disagree, both for the party and in life in general. Their disagreement over the bill was only one example. Of course, they had not so much disagreed as agreed to consider each other's points, and she was certain Thomas would vote his conscience. She could not imagine anyone, even someone as pushy as Viscount Darton, swaying him from a course of action he felt to be right. She was surprised to find, however, that he had actually had some impact on the viscount.

"I must apologize to you about my comment at the regent's dinner," Court had told her only yesterday as she worked in the garden. "I did not realize at the time how strongly you felt on the matter, nor how well informed you were."

"Would you have acted differently if you had known?" Margaret asked, surprised.

He pursed his lips thoughtfully before answering. "Perhaps not. I will not deny I dislike being bested, Miss Munroe, at politics or horse racing."

She smiled at his confession. "So I noticed."

He smiled as well, lighting the iron eyes with something approaching warmth. "Lord DeGuis is going to help me redraft the bill." He paused before adding, "If you have other points, perhaps I should hear them."

He wasn't ready to ask her advice on the rewording, but she recognized the effort he was making. "Whenever you're ready, Lord Darton, I'd be happy to discuss the matter."

She was equally happy to discuss matters with Thomas as she tried to understand him better. She had wondered, for instance, whether he overlooked his faith, mechanically attending church like so many others of their generation. She found that, like her, he listened intently to the sermon and considered it carefully afterward. They had discussed the sermon together the last couple of Sundays and again, while they could not agree on every point, they could agree to disagree peacefully, and both seemed inspired by the debate.

That they were both bruising riders she already knew, but she also found they both enjoyed swift carriage rides and quiet walks along the lake shore, rowing across the still waters, and staring into the flames of a warm fire. He preferred the more melancholy of Shakespeare's plays like *Hamlet* and *Richard III*; she preferred more active ones with humor like *The Tempest* and *A Midsummer Night's Dream*. Still, they both agreed that the Bard's work was powerful and timeless. All in all, she had every hope that indeed Thomas would make an excellent companion in life. It remained to be seen whether he would make an excellent husband.

She still could not understand his reluctance to kiss her. She had gone over the possible reasons time and again in her mind, but nothing made sense. It could not be propriety, for he was willing to hold her close and kiss her hand. It could not be that he found her undesirable; she had seen the passion flame in his eyes and felt the answering heat in her own body. For the same reason, it could not be that he was cold. Certainly his entire family was reserved. She had come to realize Catherine hid behind the trait to keep others at a distance. Lady Agnes, on the other hand only argued to hide the fact that she was not sure how else to converse. In Thomas' case, however, she could not imagine what the issue was, but knew that it was indeed a problem if he continued to refuse to discuss the matter with her.

And refuse he did. She had made several valiant attempts, only to be thwarted. As the day of the party neared, however, she had too much on her mind to pursue the matter more earnestly. She had to finalize the decorations, which included some of her carefully tended flowers in natural groupings strewn about the sitting room, dining room, and withdrawing room. She had to order the extra supplies from Hilton as well as additional footmen to serve. She also took the liberty of convincing the local baker to assist Mrs. Tate in the kitchen that evening. In her weeks at Hillwater, Margaret had learned that the thin housekeeper had several trademark dishes, but anything beyond those was nearly inedible. Accordingly, Margaret had crafted a menu that included several kinds of fish and various lamb dishes, with the opening course being Mrs. Tate's fish chowder. Everyone had assured her it was Thomas' favorite.

"It's the heavy cream," Mrs. Tate confided to Margaret in her squeaky voice. "Makes it thick and rich. Some folks claim they get dyspepsia from it, but his lordship adores it."

Margaret certainly hoped the woman was wrong about the dyspepsia. Her father had gotten an attack once when her stepmother had given a particularly elaborate dinner party. He had doubled in pain and she had flown to get a physician, thinking he was dying. The attack, thankfully, had been short-lived, and her stepmother had been careful not to include so many rich foods again. All Margaret needed was to sicken Thomas' guests. But as everyone seemed to rave about the dish, she simply had to include it.

Most important of her many duties, she had to find suitable birthday presents for the guests of honor. This proved to be another challenge, as the little village of Hilton did not boast many shopping opportunities outside dry goods and fresh produce. She persuaded Thomas to take her to Windermere, dragging him through any number of shops before deciding upon a book for Catherine.

"Lord Byron's *The Corsair*?" Thomas questioned. "Isn't that rather impassioned reading for my sister?"

"Trust me," Margaret replied. "It is exactly what she needs. It is suitably melodramatic and full of phrases that roll off the tongue. With any luck, we will have her declaiming as brightly as Lady Agnes."

Thomas looked dubious, but it was her choice for his aunt that made him raise an eyebrow.

"A parrot?" He regarded the rather motley fellow that hung in a gilded cage at the local emporium. "What on earth would she do with a parrot?"

"Parrots are often kept by the elderly," proclaimed the shop owner, a portly fellow with narrow eyes. "They provide company and conversation for those alone in the world."

"My aunt is hardly alone," Thomas informed him. Raising his quizzing glass was sufficient to send the fellow bowing hastily back to his post behind the counter.

"No," Margaret agreed, eyeing the bird who returned her gaze with a wicked black eye. "But she does enjoy conversation." She raised her voice to the proprietor. "Does he speak?"

"Actually, no," the man confessed, keeping a wary distance from Thomas. "But I'm sure he could learn, given a good model of discussion."

"There," Margaret proclaimed to Thomas. "Your aunt will have finally met someone who cannot escape her."

Thomas quirked a smile and agreed to help fund the purchase.

"Well chosen," he commented on the drive home, with the parrot carefully stowed behind the curricle. "I would not have thought of either of those, but you seem to have judged their tastes exactly. I wish I had your flair with gifts."

"You have known them longer than I have," Margaret replied, even as she blushed under his praise. "I would think that would allow you to pick even more appropriate gifts."

"If I am that able, it is only because you have opened my eyes," he told her. "I've learned a great deal from you, Margaret, and for that I will always be grateful."

Even though the words were kind, they chilled her and she pulled her shawl more closely about her shoulders. He made it sound as if he expected her to leave him soon. For once, she did not feel comfortable questioning him.

They managed to smuggle the parrot into the house and Thomas' bedchamber. Thomas, of course, would not allow her past the doorway, although she did get a brief glimpse of a room not unlike her own in its simple elegance. "Another time," he promised with a wink that set her blushing again. She could not help the fact that her heart was singing as she returned to her own bedchamber.

It was not until she took off her shawl and bonnet that she saw the letter lying on her bed. The room seemed suddenly darker, and she pulled the shawl back out of the wardrobe for warmth. Draping it about her shoulders, she moved slowly to the bed and stood looking down at the missive. From the handwriting, she knew it was from her cousin Allison.

Margaret sank onto the bed and picked up the letter with hands that barely shook. This was it. She was about to learn the mystery of Thomas' reticence, his character flaw, his secret that had alienated him from two other women who had seemed to care for him. Of course, they had clearly not cared for him as much as she did, or they would not have refused him. She wanted that fact to make a difference, but feared it would not.

Perhaps it was better not to know. Perhaps she should simply throw the letter away unread and let whatever would happen take its course. She was too honest for that. She broke the seal and spread the paper out before her.

"Dear Margaret," it read in her cousin's rounded hand. "I was indeed surprised to hear that you had been approached by the Marquis DeGuis. You must promise to tell me when next we meet how this came about. I can only hope that he is the one with whom you had fallen in love. It would certainly explain why you refused to name him, particularly as I was engaged to him at the time.

"As to Lady Janice's test, she believes in the physical demonstration of love."

Margaret paused in her reading. A physical demonstration of love? The mind boggled. She tried to picture Thomas seducing Lady Janice and shook the vision aside. Even Janice would not be so bold. She had had dozens of suitors, after all! The test could only be a kiss. And Thomas had failed. He had been unable to kiss Janice even as he was unable to kiss her. It was no doubt a result of his reticence, his infernal composure.

She picked the letter up to finish it.

"I do not believe in this physical demonstration as fully as she does," her cousin continued. "It took more than a simple kiss to convince me to marry my Geoffrey. From him I learned that love is more a combination of admiration, compatibility, and a sharing of one's most precious thoughts and dreams. If you and the marquis share such a bond, by all means, marry him. Do not distress yourself over what his past courtships might have found or not. It is your relationship with him that matters.

"I look forward to dancing at your wedding reception. I have no doubt that even should it be a breakfast, you will find a way to have dancing. Love always, your cousin Allison."

Margaret refolded the letter. Cousin Allison said look to the relationship. And what was her relationship with Thomas? Admiration, certainly, and a level of compatibility. Yet it was she who had been reticent in sharing her dreams. She realized with a pang that she had set him on a pedestal, demanding that he live up to her preconceived notions of the perfect man rather than allowing him to have very human faults. Even when he had chided her with it after the incident at Comfort House, she had been unwilling to take the issue seriously. Like Aeolus, she had formed a judgment and refused to see that the facts did not support it.

Yet, like Nicodemus, Thomas was skittish. She had been quick to judge there as well. She had condemned him for jumping too quickly from one relationship to another, yet she had not seen the effort it cost him. Small wonder he was unwilling to show his feelings. How could he possibly open his bruised heart to a woman who was impulsive, brutally honest, and oblivious to his concerns?

But now that she saw them, what could she do? There had to be a way to prove to him she loved him, that his heart would be safe with her. Simply telling him would not be enough. Surely he needed a demonstration, just as she had expected him to demonstrate his love for her.

And there lay the biggest problem of all. Even if she succeeded in showing him she loved him, would he admit that he returned her love? Or was his wounded heart simply an excuse to keep her at a distance?

Twenty-one

Margaret thought a great deal about her dilemma over the next few days as she finished the preparations for the party. She did not want to do anything that would spoil the evening she had designed for Lady Agnes and Lady Catherine. On the other hand, knowing what she knew now, she did not think she could stand to wait any longer than the party to confront Thomas. She was so busy ruminating and preparing that she paid little attention to the preparations she should be making for her own wardrobe. Her stepmother was another story, pouncing upon her and dragging her off one afternoon to decide on what she would wear to the important event.

"Truly, madame," Margaret told her when they reached the bedchamber and her stepmother had announced her intent, "I don't care. One dress is as good as another. You pick one."

Helen eyed her. "Really? But you seldom agree with my choice."

Margaret shrugged, mentally making a list of all the things she had yet to do. "I'm sure whatever you choose will be fine."

Mrs. Munroe brightened, trotting to the wardrobe and running her hands gleefully through Margaret's gowns. Margaret wandered to the window and gazed out at the front lawn in her first quiet moment since reading Allison's letter. By tomorrow night, she would have declared her love for Thomas. What if she was wrong and he didn't care? What if he was unable to care? Just the thought of it set her stomach in knots. Behind her, she suddenly noticed there was silence. Turning, she found her stepmother staring at her.

"Is something wrong, Margaret?"

Margaret struggled with her conscience. This of all times was surely the time to lie. There was no reason to worry her stepmother, especially for something over which Helen had no influence. But looking at the puckered face, she slumped in defeat. "I heard from Cousin Allison," she confessed.

Mrs. Munroe's eyes widened, and she went so far as to drop the pink sarcenet and hurry to Margaret's side. "What did she say? Is he a woman-beater?"

Margaret shook her head. "Of course not. Can you be this whole time in his company and still think that?"

"No," her stepmother acknowledged with a blush. "If I truly thought so I would not allow you to be alone with him. But in truth I cannot see there is a single thing wrong with the man. What did your cousin say?"

"She intimated that Thomas was unable to physically show his emotions."

"Oh, is that all?" Her stepmother shook her head and turned back to the wardrobe. "Honestly, the things that put off young ladies these days. Which do you think brings your eyes out to advantage—the violet silk or the sky-blue satin?"

Margaret stared at her. "Can you so easily dismiss what I said?"

"What did you say?" Helen asked. "I did not think we were discussing gowns. You left the choice to me."

"Not about gowns," Margaret snapped in exasperation. "About the Marquis DeGuis. He may be cold. He may not be able to demonstrate his love."

Mrs. Munroe shrugged. "Certainly it is an annoyance, but not a complete surprise, love. The DeGuis are noted for their composure. I'm certain he will be a kind and companionable husband for you."

Margaret made a gagging noise, and her stepmother scowled at her. "Kind? Companionable? Have you so little understanding of me, madame, that you think I would settle for such things?"

"Now you listen to me, Margaret Munroe," her stepmother declared, striding back to her side and reaching up to take Margaret's face in her hands. "Against all odds it looks as if you have won the affections, hidden though they may be, of one of the most sought-after bachelors the ton has ever produced. Need I remind you of all his excellent characteristics?"

Margaret shook her off. "No, for I am sick of hearing how wealthy he is. That doesn't matter to me. I love him, and I want him to love me in return."

Her stepmother sighed. "I'm sorry to hear your heart is so engaged. Everything tells me he cannot match your love. But I'm sure you will grow accustomed to him, Margaret."

"Accustomed." Margaret closed her eyes against the word and the vision it conjured. She could see herself withering into someone as quiet and introspective as Lady Catherine, eaten away with bitterness for the love she could never have. She opened her eyes. "No, madame, I can never grow accustomed to living without love. I'm going to show Thomas I love him. If he cannot show he loves me in return, I will break off our connection."

Her stepmother whitened. "Margaret, please, think of your future. You may never have a suitor like this again."

"I may never have any suitor again," Margaret replied logically though in truth her heart ached thinking of forcing Thomas from her life. "That does not matter. I have tried to live my life according to a set of principles, principles that include honesty and integrity. Perhaps, even with Comfort House, I have been playing the game. It is now real. This is the most important decision I have ever made, very likely the most important one I will ever make. And it is mine, madame. I thank you for your concern, but nothing you say will dissuade me."

For a moment she thought her stepmother would argue with her. She stood stiffly, head high, trying unsuccessfully to meet Margaret's gaze straight on. After a few seconds, she wilted, throwing her arms about Margaret and hugging her fiercely. "I know you will do what is right," she murmured. "Much as I want a good match for you, you would not be the woman I know if you were not true to your feelings."

Margaret hugged her in return, tears pooling at the unexpected praise. "Thank you."

Her stepmother straightened. "And now," she declared, "I still want to know—sky-blue satin or violet silk?"

A laugh bubbled up inside Margaret's tears. "Violet silk. And I'm sure you will be delighted to pick the jewelry to go with it."

Mrs. Munroe was quite delighted, gleefully returning to the wardrobe. Margaret wished her mind was so easily occupied. After her conversation with her stepmother, the party seemed an ominous affair. She wanted only to get it over with.

By the night of the event, she had to own she was a little nervous. If having Thomas on her mind was not enough, she also had to make sure everything went as planned. She was certain she must have forgotten something. Then the knocker sounded and she knew it was too late. Their guests arrived on time and in little groups that allowed introductions and conversation before the next arrived. Thomas had requested that Margaret join him and his family in the entryway to greet the guests, a gesture that should have warmed her but only made her feel more nervous. She felt like a target and waited for their guests to prove it. Fortunately, she liked the Rothbottoms right away. Lord Rothbottom was tall and angular, with a jutting chin and a severe under bite that reminded her of Aeolus when he chomped the bit. His lordship was just as eager to introduce each of his fresh-from-the-schoolroom daughters to Thomas and Court. The equally angular Lady Rothbottom was no less eager, giggling in a manner just as girlish as her daughters, and batting blue eyes innocently as if she were a maiden herself. All four daughters were tall, thin, and blond, ranging in age from fifteen to eighteen. Margaret approved of the oldest daughter's forthright manner, but the younger three, who seemed to like to remain in a huddled clump of simpering, made her wonder about the potential success of the party. Catherine's smile as she greeted them was wooden.

But then, Catherine had been even more quiet than usual the last couple of days. Margaret had thought it was the anxiety about the approaching

party and had done her best to assure Catherine that
the event was being planned for her enjoyment. The
woman had merely nodded and murmured something short but appropriate before hurrying off to
be by herself. To Margaret, it was only another sign
that the DeGuis did indeed keep everything too
much inside.

Now, watching Catherine greet the portly vicar and
his equally portly wife, she wondered whether
Thomas' sister would be able to survive the evening.
Liberal use of powder could not completely hide the
dark shadows beneath her eyes, and when she
thought no one was watching, the forced smile would
fade into something far less amenable. Margaret did
not know what to do to help the woman. She could
only hope that some of the activities she had planned
for that evening would cheer her.

The Byerslys were last to arrive. They were plumply
respectable—round and comfortable like two robins
on a fence. Their stilted response to the introductions made her wonder whether they would be worth
anything more than a five-minute conversation.
Their gangly son was greeted by a chorus of giggles
from the Rothbottom girls who waited near the sitting room door, but as he fixed his gaze in the center
of Margaret's bosom as he gushed his pleasure at
meeting her, the young ladies were doomed to disappointment. Margaret was glad when Thomas
reached out to seize the fellow and propel him into
the sitting room before he started drooling.

The Byerslys' guest was the last through the door.
Margaret chilled at the sight of him.

"Good evening, Margaret." Reggie bowed, grinning. He straightened and went so far as to wink at
Thomas, who had returned from escorting Matthew

Byersly into the clutches of the Rothbottom girls. "And good evening to you as well, my Lord DeGuis."

"Do you know this mushroom?" Lady Agnes demanded of Margaret, even as Thomas gave the fellow the barest of nods in acknowledgment.

"Know me?" Reggie gurgled before Margaret could answer. "Dear lady, we are cousins."

"By marriage," Margaret amended, seeing her carefully planned party disintegrating before her eyes. How could anyone enjoy themselves with Reggie spying on every action? How could she get Thomas alone if her cousin was watching her every move? Small wonder the Byerslys were closed-mouthed; they had no other defense if they were silly enough to invite Reggie to stay with them.

Reggie ignored her implied slur. "And I was the one to introduce her to his lordship."

"Well, at least you have one good deed to your credit," Lady Agnes quipped.

To Margaret's relief, Thomas interceded to introduce his aunt and sister. Her relief was short-lived, however, as no sooner had Reggie bowed gushing over their hands than he grabbed her arm as if to lead her into the sitting room.

"We have much to discuss, cousin," he said, beaming. Margaret's heart sank. She should shake him off and tell him to take himself home, but she had promised herself to be on her best behavior.

Thomas loomed up to block their way. He removed Reggie's arm from hers. "Sorry, Pinstin. Your discussion will have to wait. Miss Munroe is acting as my hostess tonight. I'm sure you'll understand."

Reggie began sputtering something that sounded suspiciously like congratulations but Thomas whisked Margaret away into the sitting room before she could be sure.

"Thank you for the rescue," she murmured, enjoying the feel of his arm under hers and wondering whether it would be the last time she felt it.

"My pleasure," Thomas assured her, casting a glance at her cousin, who was greeting her father and stepmother. "Lord knows I've needed rescuing from the fellow often enough. Someday I'm going to feel compelled to strike him, I fear."

Margaret stared at him, but his face was as composed as always. Even in his dislikes, he showed no emotion. She was doomed.

Dinner, however, went well. The vicar said the blessing in his considered, respectful voice, and everyone made congenial conversation. Reggie told several *on-dits* that set the Byerslys, Rothbottoms, and even Court laughing. Seated next to Thomas, with Court on her right, only Catherine was quiet. Thomas, on the other hand, was plainly pleased with the meal. Margaret did not think she had ever seen him eat so much as he did of the fish chowder. Still, even though he clearly delighted in it, his face was composed and he took each bite politely, never showing how much he cared for it. The fact set her spirits plummeting once again.

The presentation of the gifts, on the other hand, raised them. Catherine paled at the love poem, but thanked her kindly for it. By the way she kept running her gloved hands over the tooled leather cover, Margaret knew she liked it. Reggie opened his mouth as if to make a witty comment, and Margaret glared him into silence.

Lady Agnes was even more obviously pleased with her gift. She crowed in delight at the parrot.

"He doesn't talk yet," Margaret explained when Thomas' aunt had tried immediately to engage it in conversation. "But I expect you will enjoy teaching him a few terms."

"He might even learn to debate you," Mr. Munroe put in.

Lady Agnes eyed the colorful bird thoughtfully. "He might indeed. Aren't there certain terms used in debate in Parliament? Did you ever learn those, Thomas?"

Thomas quirked a smile, winking at Margaret even as Court frowned at how his aunt would unknowingly disparage him. "I think I may remember a few. If I can't remember, I'm sure Viscount Darton can be of assistance. We would be delighted to help you teach the bird."

Court agreed good naturedly.

Lady Agnes was eager to start, but other amusements awaited. They all wandered in companionable conversation to the withdrawing room. As they entered, the quartet began a gentle melody. Lord Rothbottom grinned. Matthew Bylersly sidled up to Margaret and cleared his throat. Court bowed to Catherine.

"Might I have the honor of the first dance on your birthday, Lady Catherine?"

This, of course, proved to be nearly the party's demise.

"No, thank you, Lord Darton," Catherine replied, turning away from everyone. "I find myself fatigued. Please enjoy yourselves without me." She walked to the windows while most of her guests gazed at each other, perplexed. Reggie's gleaming eyes told Margaret he was memorizing the moment for future use. Court's mouth tightened, but he turned gallantly to Lady Agnes. "Perhaps you might be willing to take your niece's place, my lady?"

Lady Agnes was too busy frowning after Catherine. "No, thank you."

Court bowed, stiffly. When he straightened, it was to find the oldest Rothbottom girl in front of him, batting her lashes in obvious expectation. Unable to escape with any form of politeness, he offered her his arm and she grabbed it as a drowning victim grabs a lifeline. He gave Thomas a dark look as he led her onto the floor.

The vicar and his wife demurred, but Lord and Lady Rothbottom took the floor, as did Mr. and Mrs. Munroe. Reggie, of course, was content to watch, and Margaret could only hope he would have the sense to leave Catherine alone. Thomas bowed to Margaret, and they completed the set. The others took seats about the room to watch.

Margaret tried to enjoy the dance, but every few turns brought Catherine into view, and guilt stabbed her. The woman stared out the window into the darkening night, head bowed, and mouth turned down in melancholy. If Margaret had succeeded in giving her a memorable birthday, no one would have guessed. It did not seem right that the guest of honor should be so downcast. As soon as the last bars of the music faded, she excused herself from a surprised Thomas and hurried to the girl's side, ignoring the interested glances her cousin cast her.

"You don't have to dance with Lord Darton, you know," she told Catherine. "If you asked, I'm sure my father would partner you."

Catherine managed a smile, turning from the window. "That would be kind of him, but I'm not overly fond of dancing."

"But this is your party," Margaret insisted. "You told me you wanted dancing. If it does not amuse you, what would you like to do?"

Catherine glanced about in an obvious attempt to make sure no one else was in hearing distance. "Can you help me go outside to meet Christien?"

"He's here?" Margaret yelped. Then, hastily lowering her voice as Reggie pricked up his ears, she added, "He followed you from London?"

Catherine nodded. "I begged him to. The summer was too long without him. I've managed to slip away a few times since he arrived, but not for the last couple of days. Could you help me?"

Margaret cocked her head. "What about simply telling Thomas instead? It is your birthday. Perhaps he would be inclined to grant you a wish."

"I doubt that," Catherine replied, wringing her hands. "I told Christien of your advice about Thomas, and he agreed it was too dangerous."

"Did he?" Margaret frowned suspiciously. "And what did he advise, a hasty trip to Gretna Green?"

"No." Catherine shuddered. "He told me to accept Lord Darton's offer. He is so noble! I cannot do it, Miss Munroe. I fear I am not as strong as he is. I cannot stand waiting any longer. I have a plan."

"I'm almost afraid to hear it," Margaret replied. "I simply do not understand why you cannot be honest with your brother. I know he loves you."

Catherine picked at the skirt of her rose-colored dress. "I believe he loves me, but he also wants what he thinks is best for me. That is why I intend to prove to him that Christien is best."

"And how are you going to do that when you cannot even admit the fellow exists?" Margaret demanded.

Catherine glanced up at her, deep blue eyes determined. "I will arrange for Thomas to see Lord Darton trying to take liberties, only Christien will arrive to save me before it is too late."

"That is the most ridiculous thing I have ever heard," Margaret declared, exasperated. "In the first place, Lord Darton is not likely to act the libertine knowing your brother is nearby. In the second, while you might get Thomas to agree that Darton is not the best man for you, it does not follow that Christien is."

"But it will work!" Catherine cried. "It must work! I cannot bear being away from him! These last few days have been impossible. I feel I will burst under the strain."

Margaret could well imagine that. "Then talk to Thomas," she ordered.

"Talk to Thomas about what?" Thomas asked politely behind her. Behind him, Reggie was panting with eagerness.

Catherine washed white. Margaret smiled sweetly. "A very important matter, I assure you. If you'll excuse me, I'll let your sister explain." With a warning glanced at the wide-eyed and trembling Catherine, she left her to Thomas' curious attentions, grabbing Reggie's arm to steer him away. She only hoped the girl would do the right thing and confess, before she caused a great deal of trouble, for everyone.

Twenty-two

Thomas had in fact come in search of Margaret. As soon as he had her in custody, he intended to signal the quartet to begin a waltz. He still had only seen the dance performed, but felt himself capable of trying, especially given the significance of the act. Surely she would remember her father had said he might propose once he proved he could waltz. The DeGuis diamond lay heavy in his pocket of his black and white striped waistcoat. As he looked at Margaret with his sister, he was a little surprised to find his palms sweating inside his gloves. He was about to make a statement that would tie him to Margaret for eternity. Funny how he had never felt this nervous in his first two courtships.

Now, much as he would have liked to protest Margaret's departure, however, he could easily see that something was upsetting Catherine. Accordingly, he let Margaret go without a murmur and focused on his sister.

"What is it, Catherine?" he asked gently.

She swallowed, avoided his gaze, and began wringing her hands. "Oh, Thomas, I don't know how to begin."

Alarmed, he caught her hands in his own. "Whatever it is is obviously of great concern to you. Therefore, it is of great concern to me. Please, tell me."

She looked up and immediately flinched. "Everyone's watching us!"

Glancing over his shoulder, he saw she was right. Even though Margaret had drawn off Pinstin, the fellow was still gazing at Catherine. Lord and Lady Rothbottom had paused in their conversation with the Byerslys. Lady Agnes was frowning in his direction. Even the simpering Rothbottom chit was peering over the top of her fan in curiosity. A few weeks ago he would have told his sister to pull herself together before she made a scene. That was before Margaret had shown him how superficial his life was. Turning back to Catherine, he offered her his arm.

"If you need someone to talk with, Catherine," he told her, "I am quite willing. Perhaps a stroll in the gardens will give us the privacy you need."

She accepted his arm, but his suggestion only seemed to worry her further. "No! That is, we do not need to go outside. Perhaps a simple promenade would do."

He nodded, leading her forward. The musicians were looking in his direction and he shook his head. They launched into a lively gavotte. The Rothbottoms and Byerslys returned to the floor. Court, still attempting to escape the determined young ladies, offered for a surprised Margaret, who was clearly torn. He smiled wryly at her dilemma—enjoying her beloved dancing or keeping Pinstin from poisoning her party. She shook her head at Court and dragged her protesting cousin onto the floor. Court strode out into the garden to escape. The Byersly son offered for the youngest Rothbottom girl, which annoyed her older sisters, if the rapid plying of fans was any indication.

"Now, then," he said to his sister as the dancers began to move. "What seems to be the trouble?"

She tried to start several times, trailing off lamely after the first word. He gathered it had something to do with Court and the marriage business, and gave her arm a squeeze.

"I've told you repeatedly you do not have to marry the viscount," he chided. "Am I such an ogre to force you?"

She glanced up at him and quickly away, biting her lip before answering him. "I don't know. I've never felt the need to stand up to you before, Thomas. I'm not sure I can. Will you truly listen to me if I say I will not marry him?"

Thomas sighed. "I've done all I can, Catherine. You do not seem to have grown accustomed to him, as I had hoped. Court does not seem overly enthused either, if that is any comfort. I obviously chose the wrong person for you. I'll tell him the marriage is off."

She let out her breath slowly as if she had been holding it for some time. "Thank you, Thomas."

"I told you, I'm not an ogre," he replied, still a little stung that she would think him so unfeeling. But then, perhaps he had been unfeeling before Margaret had shown him the error of his ways. His eyes sought out Margaret, gracefully darting through the dance. Reggie had more appreciation for the drama with Catherine than for his cousin's talents. Thomas wished he could take the fellow's place. As he watched, Margaret looked up at him and grinned. He smiled in return.

"Everyone should find a soul mate," he told Catherine. "We'll find someone for you, as soon as we return to town. I promise you, you will have your own establishment before the end of the next Season."

She faltered in her steps. They were just passing Lady Agnes, who scowled at him in her debate with Mr. Munroe. Mrs. Munroe was frowning as well. Thomas' smile froze into a polite mask.

"I don't want you to find someone else," Catherine all but whined. "I will not marry anyone just because you set him before me!"

Her tone was rising again, and despite his good intentions, he frowned.

"I don't intend to offer you gentlemen on a platter, like a tray of sweetmeats," he replied. "I think we should be able to have a civil discussion about the matter this time."

She pulled up short, not far from the end of the dance floor, requiring him to stop as well. He had never seen his sister so agitated. Bright color spotted her cheeks and her eyes blazed. "This isn't a debate in Parliament, Thomas, or a discussion with your man of business as to what you should invest on the Exchange. This is my life. And I am tired of you interfering in it!"

His guests were beginning to stare again, and this time, Thomas felt his temper rising. It would do his family and his heart no good for him to snap now. He struggled to contain the frustration, snapping out his words against the building anger. "I do not consider wishing to see my sister happy interference. Or are you complaining about the homes I have set up for you, the food I provide, your wardrobe?"

"As if those mattered!" She sneered. Another time he would have marveled that her temper was as volatile as his, but at the moment, all he could do was grit his teeth.

"I daresay they matter to some people."

"Not to me," she declared. "All I've ever wanted, Thomas, was for someone to appreciate and love me, just as I am. You can't seem to do that. I feel as if you're constantly poking at me to be something I'm not."

"I've never done that," he argued vehemently. "All I've asked is that you be a DeGuis. That name comes with a certain level of expectation."

"Oh!" she squealed. "I'm so sick of that! What makes us so special? Why are we the model to which all others aspire? I cringe every time Aunt Agnes says that. You may be perfect, Thomas, but I cannot, I will not live up to your ideal of perfection. I do not want to keep everything inside me. I want to shout if I'm angry. I want to cry if I'm sad. I don't want to pretend I'm stunningly beautiful, or witty, or vivacious, when I'm none of those things. I'm not even as honest as your Margaret Munroe."

"The last person you should compare yourself to," Thomas all but shouted, "is Margaret Munroe."

The name echoed in the silent room. Catherine glared at him, bosom heaving. The music had stopped, all conversation had ceased. Every person in the room was staring at him. He was the center of attention, the thing he most despised. Worse, the comment, which everyone had clearly heard, could be taken as publicly disparaging the woman he loved.

The woman he loved.

He was an idiot not to have seen it before. How could he not fall in love with a woman who was loving and giving, who gave her heart willingly even as he kept his sheltered. He turned slowly and met Margaret's gaze. Her face was puckered and pale, but instead of accusation or anger in her blue eyes, he saw sadness. She was disappointed in him. She had every right to be. His gut clenched.

He started forward, and Catherine caught his arm. "Thomas, I . . ." she began. He shrugged her off.

"Not now, Catherine. We've done enough damage for one night. I'll talk with you later." He started forward again. Lady Agnes scowled at him. His other guests eyed the tableau in varying states of amazement and amusement. Even Reggie looked stunned. Mr. Munroe shook his clearly distressed wife off his arm and moved to intercept him. Thomas waved him away. The musicians, seeing his movement toward the lady, began the unmistakable strains of a waltz. Margaret bolted across the room and out the double doors to the verandah. Thomas could only follow.

He pulled up short at the steps down into the garden. The light was dimming, and amidst the riotous blooms, he did not see her immediately.

"Shall I fetch her for you, my lord?" Pinstin panted at his elbow. "She is my cousin, after all, and if I do say so myself, I know the way to handle her properly."

Thomas took both his hands and grabbed Reggie by the lapels of his navy velvet coat, lifting the fellow to the toes of his evening pumps. "I've had about all I can take tonight, Pinstin. This is between the lady and myself. You will return to the house and you will mention nothing of this evening to anyone or so help me God, cousin or no, I will thrash you within an inch of your worthless life. Do I make myself clear?"

"Perfectly," Reggie squeaked, eyes bulging in obvious fear.

Thomas dropped him and turned his gaze to the garden. Reggie gulped and fled.

I'm overwrought, Thomas thought, scanning the grounds. *I've been an idiot in so many ways. Cranwell was right—it does no one any good to bury their emotions. No more.* He spotted a shadow amongst the roses and wound his way to Margaret's side.

"Go away," she said before he was closer than five feet.

"To the point as always," he tried teasing, edging closer.

"Would you like it wrapped up in sugar? Go away, please."

"No," he replied, succeeding in reaching her side. He put out a hand to touch her shoulder, and she shrugged him away.

"Oh, whyever not?" she demanded, turning her back on him. "You've made your feelings abundantly clear, at last. And I was afraid you could not do so. I suppose I should have expected this outcome. Were you trying to be kind before? Were you going to wait out the whole summer to tell me you had determined we will not suit?"

"Won't you let me explain?" Thomas tried, racking his brain for a way to do just that.

"No," she repeated. "There is nothing to explain. For whatever reason, you have finally decided that the perfect Thomas DeGuis cannot marry a notorious Original like Margaret Munroe. No one will fault you. I imagine some like Lord Darton will celebrate."

"I am not perfect," he replied. "And I have not decided we do not suit. I think we suit, admirably. I cannot imagine a more delightful companion in life." He pulled the DeGuis diamond from his pocket. "I had intended to do this another way, but my own foolishness prevented it. Margaret Munroe, will you marry me?"

She gasped, whirling to stare at him. He could see the sparkle of tears on her cheeks. He offered her a smile, conscious of the way his heart was suddenly hammering inside his rib cage, as fast and furious as the hooves of their horses when they raced. But if he died that moment, it would be worth it to know she accepted him. She continued to stare for a moment, as if doubting what she had heard, then her gaze dropped to the diamond in his grip.

"What is that?" she asked.

He took her left hand and carefully slid it over the glove onto her fourth finger. "The DeGuis diamond. It is customary to give it to the bride-to-be when proposing."

She stared at it another moment before cocking her head to glance up at him. "Are you sure about this, Thomas?" she asked. "You didn't exactly sound proud of me a moment ago. You don't have to offer yourself as an apology."

"What I meant inside," he told her, "was that Catherine should not be comparing herself to you because you are one of a kind. No woman could possibly match you."

She narrowed her eyes. "What a kind explanation. From anyone else, I'd think it a lie."

"Have I ever lied to you?"

She took a deep breath. "No, never." Glancing down at the ring, she bit her lip, and dark spots appeared on her glove, stains from her renewed crying. Moved, he pulled her into his arms.

"I am quite serious, Margaret," he murmured into her hair. "I want you to marry me. I can think of no finer woman to have by my side. Please believe me."

"I'd be delighted to," she hiccoughed through her crying. She raised her head and gazed at him, eyes luminous. "If you would just kiss me."

Twenty-three

Margaret gazed up at him, heart racing. Surely now, having proposed, he would kiss her. She had seen the tenderness in his eyes, deep, sweet. As she watched, doubt crept in, then fear. He was afraid to kiss her. Even now the DeGuis composure was reasserting itself. There was only one thing for it. Margaret arched up on tiptoe and kissed him.

He recoiled immediately, so that their lips barely brushed. Determined, she pursued him, throwing herself into his arms. The weight of her pressing against him put him off balance. He had no choice but to tighten his embrace, stumbling backward to fetch up against a maple. For a moment more his lips remained cold beneath hers and she could feel her despair building. Then, with a groan that either signaled surrender or annoyance, he bent his head to hers.

The kiss was as wonderful as the man she loved—warm, powerful, all-consuming. It was as if, having kept his emotions in control for so long, they burst forth in a torrent that threatened to sweep her away. He devoured her mouth, peppered kisses across her cheek, buried his lips in the hollow of her throat. She laughed aloud for the joy of it, shivering in delight. The sound had not even faded before he broke off, nearly dropping her in his haste. Even in the moon-light, she could see he had reddened.

"Forgive me," he rasped out, running the back of his hand across his swollen lips as if to wipe away the last few minutes. "I don't know what came over me. I promise you, it won't happen again."

Margaret nearly cried out in disappointment and bewilderment. Couldn't he tell how much his kiss had meant to her? Hadn't he felt the joyful response of her body? Couldn't he see the love she could feel shining in her eyes? He flinched at her look, now reproachful, and she cringed. She had lost against the DeGuis reticence. She couldn't stand to look at him.

Turning her back, she fumbled with the diamond, yanking it off her finger. It felt like a dead weight in her hand. Gathering the shreds of her wounded pride, she turned back to him and shoved out the ring.

"Here, take it," she ordered with a voice that barely shook. "Did you really think I would marry a man who cannot be intimate? The famed conse-quence of the DeGuis name means nothing. All I wanted was you."

"Margaret," he choked, refusing to accept the rock. His eyes were tortured. A perverse part of her was glad. The kinder part of her quailed. She seized his hand and slapped the diamond into it.

"Take it, Thomas. Give it to some colorless female who doesn't care." She turned on him again, feeling hot tears burning behind her eyes. He caught her arm, but before he could speak, another voice cut in.

"Unhand me! Help!"

There was a muffled cry of surprise and the thud of something heavy falling.

"Catherine?" Thomas called, frowning. Margaret rolled her eyes.

"It only wanted that!" She grabbed his hand and towed him in the direction of the call. "You must see this, Thomas. I'm sure you will appreciate it. Another DeGuis who cannot find an appropriate way to acknowledge feelings."

They stepped out of the roses to the center bench of the garden. Catherine bent over the prone figure of a young man. Court stood nearby, rubbing the knuckles of his hand and looking baffled. He straightened in obvious relief at the sight of Thomas.

"What is going on here?" Thomas demanded.

Catherine sat to cradle the young man's head in her lap. His blond curly hair was tousled, his full lower lip trickled blood, and he gazed reproachfully at Court like a puppy who's been chastised by its master. Catherine pointed a trembling finger at the viscount.

"That miscreant attacked us!"

Margaret wanted to argue, remembering the plan Catherine had described, but the blood on Christien's lip was rather convincing. Court's protest only served to reinforce the picture.

"And what was I to think? The fellow had his arms about you!"

Catherine immediately began to argue. The young man voiced his reproof, and Court crossed his arms and glowered. Thomas glanced among them, frown deepening.

"Enough," Margaret thundered. They all blinked at her, stuttering into silence. She turned to Thomas. "Your sister is in love with an itinerant French painter named Christien LaTour. That," she pointed to the man, "if I am not mistaken, is he. Be so kind as to introduce yourself, Monsieur LaTour."

Christien scrambled to his feet, tugging his worn brown coat into place and running a hand back through his hair. Catherine clung to his other arm, making his attempt at a bow impossibly awkward.

"My lords, your servant," he said in a soft tenor. "And if I may correct Miss Munroe, I am not an itinerant. I am an artist. It is only a matter of time before I find a sponsor."

"A very short time, I'm sure," Catherine murmured, large eyes worshipful. "He is gifted." He reddened under her praise.

"I believe you've met Viscount Darton," Margaret continued. "And as you've been skulking about the place for days, you must have recognized Thomas, Marquis DeGuis."

The fellow's color heightened further as Thomas scowled. He adjusted his rumpled cravat. "Mademoiselle Munroe has a unique way with words. I did not consider it 'skulking.' "

"Of course not," Catherine declared with a frown at Margaret. "After all, I invited him."

Thomas rubbed the bridge of his nose. "I am having difficulty following all this. Catherine, perhaps you should explain."

Catherine immediately paled, glancing between her brother and the man on her arm. "I . . . well . . . I don't know where to begin."

"Oh, give it up!" Margaret snapped. "You have been caught. If you could not be honest before, at least do us the honor of being so now."

Catherine's mouth puckered at the censure. Christien gave her hand a squeeze. Then he disengaged from her and stepped forward, raising his head. "Lord DeGuis, I met your sister last winter when Lady Agnes commissioned me to paint a miniature of her. We fell in love."

"Instantly," Catherine breathed in raptured confirmation.

"I see," Thomas intoned. Margaret watched him, but as usual, his face gave no indication of what he was thinking.

"Told you there was another fellow," Court interjected.

"I realize I am not worthy of your sister's hand," Christien continued. "I have urged her repeatedly to accept Lord Darton's offer of marriage. I know he will care for her."

Margaret was not surprised by Catherine's immediate protest. She was surprised to hear Court chime in just as heatedly.

"Certainly I'd care for her," he avowed. "But just as certainly, I refuse to marry a woman who loves elsewhere. I have high standards for my bride, and love, for me, is one of them."

Margaret reached out to clap him on the shoulder, startling him. "Well said, my lord! I never thought you had scruples."

He frowned. "I gather that is supposed to be a compliment?"

"Just say thank you," Thomas advised. "I find it safest." He turned to the couple. "And what do you propose now?"

"I won't marry anyone else," Catherine declared, stamping her foot and moving to recapture Christien's arm. She clung defiantly and rather possessively.

He removed her gently, but firmly. "You must marry someone else. I cannot care for you as your brother does."

She puckered again and Margaret marveled at their idiocy.

"I can see we will not resolve this tonight," Thomas

put in before she moved to intervene and as Catherine threatened tears. "Master LaTour, would you be so good as to wait on us tomorrow, say eleven? I believe I may know of a sponsor for you that would put this entire picture in a different light, if you pardon the pun."

Now Catherine turned worshipful eyes on her brother. "Oh, Thomas. I never knew you had it in you."

Thomas kept a smile on his face, though Margaret could see by the tick in his cheek that he wanted to laugh at her. "I take it back, Catherine. You are beginning to have some traits very like Miss Munroe."

"That," his sister said with a toss of her head, "I take as a compliment. My love, may I see you to the gate?"

Christien bowed to Thomas, this time gracefully, and accepted her arm. Court watched them go with a shake of his head.

"A French artist," he muttered. "Who would have thought?"

"Be a good fellow, Court," Thomas put in, "and leave us alone for a few minutes? I have something of importance to discuss with Miss Munroe."

Court coughed, hastily bowing out of the clearing. Margaret swallowed, facing him at last.

"I'm not certain I have the strength to hear what you have to say, Thomas," she told him. "I know all the reasons we do not suit. You do not like the fact that I race, you hate the waltz, you think Comfort House a shocking way to fulfill the Christian commission. Is there anything left to say?"

"Yes," he maintained, moving to capture her hands again. "Can't you see how much I've changed, Margaret? How much you've changed me? I love having you beside me when we race. I love not knowing

THE MARQUIS' KISS

whether I can beat you on any given day. I even like feeling free to maul your cousin when he annoys me. I fully intended to waltz with you tonight, and if you'll just agree to marry me, I will prove it to you in front of my family and our guests. As to Comfort House, while it does concern me that you volunteer there, it has nothing to do with whether it is the right thing to do, just as I agree with you that workhouses are not the answer. It's just that I worry for your safety. As I suspect I would not be welcome there to protect you, we will simply have to hire you a strapping footman to escort you."

Margaret smiled wryly. "It does my heart good to hear you say this, Thomas, but when all is said and done, you don't really want to marry me. That is clear. Can we not leave it at that?"

"No," he said, "we cannot. You value the truth, Margaret Munroe. It's time you heard it."

Twenty-four

Margaret steeled herself for the worst. He would finally tell her what kept him from opening his heart to her. She would finally know what kept them apart.

"It can only be our different approaches to life," she said, sounding defensive even to her own ears. "I warned you from the beginning that we were too different."

"Differences can attract as well as repel," he countered. "In truth, I am not certain I will ever get the hang of living in the moment. I was hoping to rely on you for my guide."

"I want to be more than a guide, Thomas," she chided. "I want to be your wife, your lover. I'd be a fool to discount your intelligence, your breeding, and your wealth, especially as my stepmother continually throws them in my face, but I'd cheerfully marry you without all those things if I had your love."

"You have it," he insisted, tightening his grip on her hands as if he could make her believe it. "I did not expect to fall in love, but I did. My life will be hollow if you refuse me, Margaret."

She wrenched her hands away. "Then why? Why do you persist in keeping your heart hidden?"

He wanted to tell her. He knew he had to do so. He straightened, resolving to do just that. Pain shot up from his gut to his chest, and he gasped aloud, forced to bend against it. Margaret was instantly beside him.

"Thomas, what is it?"

He shook his head, clutching his chest in an irrational hope he could somehow stop the agony. Searing heat spurted upward through his throat, and he swallowed bile. She put her arm about his shoulder.

"Take a deep breath," she advised, trying to still her own panic. "And another. Can you tell me what's wrong?"

He obeyed her, and the pain abated, leaving him as usual feeling frustrated and not a little afraid. "Sorry," he muttered as he straightened through the lingering burning. "Do not look so worried. I'm fine."

"You are most assuredly not fine," Margaret scolded him. "Did you notice the utter misery your sister went through hiding her feelings this past week? Tell me what's wrong. Is it your heart?"

He wanted to shield her, but her eyes were implacable. "I fear so," he admitted.

"How many of these attacks have you had?" She was afraid to hear the answer, but she had to know.

"Three, with the first last winter."

She frowned. "Have you seen a physician? Is there nothing that can be done?"

"I saw a physician after the first and second attacks. He thought at first it was an aberration. At the time, I must admit it was comforting. When it occurred again, he thought my heart was failing from too much exertion. He advised me to settle my courtship quickly, not," he added hurriedly before she could get the wrong impression, "that that had any bearing on my decision to propose."

She cocked her head in thought. Since she had

known him, she had heard his heart speed on several occasions, yet he had never had an attack. It made no sense that his heart was failing. "Show me where the pain is the greatest," she insisted.

That wrung a chuckle from him. "Are you a talented physician as well?" When she put her hands on her hips, he shook his head and complied, pointing to his lower left rib. Margaret's frown deepened.

"That doesn't look like your heart to me. It looks like your stomach."

He shook his head. "I've had an upset stomach once or twice in my life. This is nothing like that, I assure you."

Margaret continued to eye his gut. "Let us try an experiment." Before Thomas knew what she was about, she took both hands and pressed against his stomach. The pain shot up again, but this time, what erupted was a loud belch.

Thomas colored. "I beg your pardon."

Margaret laughed, throwing her arms about him in relief. "Oh, Thomas, don't apologize! You are not dying! I daresay you've never done anything in excess your entire life, so you would not know the symptoms of dyspepsia. I would also hazard a guess that each time these attacks occurred, you had treated yourself to an overdose of Mrs. Tate's fish chowder."

Thomas accepted her hug, stunned. Could it be so easy? "Dyspepsia? Is that all?"

She released him, grinning. "Do not sound so disappointed. I'm thoroughly glad you are not ready to stick your spoon in the wall just yet. Perhaps we might still have time to work out our differences."

Seeing the expectation in her eyes, he almost wished he could use the excuse of his near demise. He had to confess his fears, even though he knew she already had proof. He had put his heart into his kiss, as he had never done before. Feeling her willing response, as free and giving as the lady herself, had set his blood on fire. For a moment, he had dreamed of a true union, mind, heart, and soul.

Then Margaret had laughed.

He had always admired her laugh. But the sound of it then had scored him to the bone. It could only mean that he had failed yet again. Only this time, there would be no recovery. This time, he had lost not only his dignity and pride but his heart.

She stood waiting, her look a challenge. For the first time in his life, he considered running. But too much hung in the balance.

"You deserve better," he said.

Margaret's brows shot up so high they were nearly lost in her silver-veined hair. "Better?" She started to laugh and he flinched. "Better? Thomas DeGuis, who could possibly be better than you?"

He bowed his head. "I am not perfect, Margaret. I cannot resist a challenge, no matter what it cost me. And as you noticed tonight, I have a nasty temper. It takes a lot to goad me, but once goaded, I behave no better than a maddened bull. I do and say things I find abhorrent afterward."

"I cannot believe you would beat me," Margaret protested.

"No, never!" The very idea repelled him. "I promise you, Margaret, I will never raise a hand to you. My voice, however, is another matter."

She shrugged. "In truth, it is an annoyance. But I am fully capable of giving as good as I get, or of deflecting the criticism if it is unwarranted. As long as you show me you love me in other ways."

There lay the rub and the challenge. He straightened. "If you insist, I will kiss you whenever you like."

"If I insist?" She frowned. "You make it sound like an onerous chore."

"It is," he replied, watching her, "for you."

"What on earth are you talking about?" she demanded. "Thomas, I've been brazenly begging for your kiss for weeks. What makes you think I don't like it?"

"I have had . . . reports . . . that my kiss is less than delightful." There, he had said it. He waited for her agreement.

"What idiot told you that?" she cried. "Oh, let me guess. Lady Janice Willstencraft. Was that her test? A kiss?"

"Test?" Now it was Thomas' turn to frown.

"She has a test she administers to each suitor," Margaret explained. "She would not tell me what it was, for fear of her reputation. She must have exhaustingly high standards, for she must have refused a dozen men before you."

Thomas shook his head, afraid to hope. "But your cousin Allison felt the same way."

"Really?" She looked surprised. "Well, I suppose that is to be expected. She was in love with someone else."

"Would that make a difference?" he asked with equal surprise.

"Oh, Thomas," she replied, sighing wistfully, "of *course* it makes a difference!" When he still looked perplexed, she turned thoughtful. "Though I daresay it does not make a difference for some. Certainly the ladies at Comfort House would vouch for the fact that a good kiss does not require love. Yet I think any act is more enjoyable if you put your heart into it."

"I would like to put my heart into it," Thomas murmured, "if you would let me."

She swallowed, nodding, and held out her arms.

He walked stiffly into them as if going to his execution. But the smile and the light in her eyes was so tender, he knew he had come home at last. He pulled her close and kissed her.

It was some time before either could speak again. Then Margaret laughed and Thomas joined her, free and loving merriment lifting to the stars above in a prayer of thanksgiving as old as time.

"You see?" Margaret smiled at him. "The reason you kissed badly, my lord, is that you were kissing the wrong women."

"You appear to be right," he replied, returning her smile and smoothing her disheveled hair away from her forehead. "You have my heart and my love. I've never met anyone like you, Margaret Munroe."

She laughed again. "Well, of course not. I am an Original. Now, show me again how you intend to kiss me once we're married."

Then she surrendered to the joy of the marquis' kiss.

Dear Reader,

I hope you enjoyed the story of Thomas and Margaret's courtship. I love writing about different heroines, ladies who inspire us to be ourselves, often against the very potent attractions of the world around us.

I also enjoy connecting my books, as those of you who have read my previous works may have noticed. One reader requested that I mention where characters in one book appear in others. For those who are interested, Thomas's kiss to Margaret's cousin Allison is described in *Catch of the Season*. The story of what happens to Margaret's friends Robbie and Kevin Whattling is told in *The Bluestocking on His Knee*. Chas Prestwick, Margaret's racing conspirator, is the hero in *The Unflappable Miss Fairchild,* which also features Lord Leslie Petersborough, who helped her research the dreaded Poor Laws amendment. Les is one of Lady Agnes DeGuis's godchildren.

By the by, an amendment to the Poor Laws was enacted in 1834, ushering in the age of the workhouse so vividly depicted in Charles Dickens' work.

I'm always interested in hearing from my readers. You can reach me via Kensington Publishers. Please include a stamped, self-addressed envelope if you'd like a reply. Or try my web site at www.reginascott.com

Happy reading!
Regina Scott

More Zebra Regency Romances